TEXAS 2077

Also by Carlos Miralejos
Rabid Beasts

TEXAS 2077

A Futuristic Novel

CARLOS MIRALEJOS

OUTER SPACE
PRESS

Cover design by Joaquin Navarro

Hardcover price: $20.95

Please turn to the last page for ordering information

This book is a work of fiction. The characters, names, places, incidents, dialogue, and plot are the products of the author's imagination or are used fictitiously. Any resemblance to actual persons, companies or events is purely coincidental and not intended by the author.

Texas 2077

For information contact Outer Space Press, P.O. Box 9593, Daytona Beach, FL 32120.

Library of Congress Catalog Card Number: 98-65817

ISBN 0-9625266-4-9

First Edition
10 9 8 7 6 5 4 3 2 1

Please turn to the last page for ordering information.

With love for my wife Aurora

joy of my youth

mother of our children.

ACKNOWLEDGMENTS

I want to express my heartfelt gratitude to Janet M.Rogerson and Eva Jones, both colleagues from the Ormond Writers' League, for correcting my grammar and syntax, and for criticizing the story portrayed in the book. I'm also grateful to my editor, DanaRae Pomeroy.

Contents

51,829 Words

Part One - 1999

1 Echoes From The Past

Wednesday, 14 April 1999

Familiar with the route to Orlando's International Airport from his office at C. Kirby Enterprises, David was startled to realize he'd missed the interchange with I-4. He had no excuse other than he became absent-minded, thinking about the way C.K. upper management handled racial relations, and how their image makers manipulated them.

He turned off W. International Drive onto Vineland Road, and caught I-4 eastward, toward the interchange with the Beeline Expressway. He hated to pay the tolls, but it was the quickest way to the Airport.

David drove his new 1999 Chrysler Concord up the spiraling ramp of the parking facility, not bothering to look for a parking space at the lower levels. Instead, he went straight to the top; there, under the scorching Florida sun, he quickly found a parking space.

Texas 2077

David checked the big board in the main waiting area. Jean's flight was on time, 3:25 P.M. After passing the metal detector stations, he hurried by a flock of incoming travelers, getting off the shuttle between the arrival gates and the main terminal building. He barely made the next train leaving for the arrival gates. Once there, he rushed to gate 27, the gate assigned to Jean's flight.

Anxiously, David waited by the gate's door. After a couple of minutes, he spotted his girl friend walking on the jetway corridor.

"Jean! " called David, waving to her.

"How long have you being waiting, sweetie?" asked Jean, after kissing him.

"Only a couple of minutes. How were things in L.A.?"

"Oh...not too bad, I guess."

They made their way to the baggage claim area, then Jean explained. "Last Monday, I had a meeting with Cliff Miller, the big honcho at Double Reel Films Corporation."

"Really...what happened?"

"I presented our case and our concerns. He didn't like it at all. In fact, he said that Double Reel production and staffing policies were none of my business."

"That son of a bitch doesn't give a damn about anything, except money."

David realized he'd impulsively blurted out an old cliche and quickly added, "Actually, it's more than money. He belongs to a clan of business and religious leaders that are manipulating TV shows, media coverage of sport events, movies, and even the news, with the purpose of influencing who gets to be famous and well-liked. They want to control the country's soul. They're afraid of the future and decided to act now, before it's too late."

"There it is, that one's my bag." Jean pointed to a big, light-brown suitcase.

David retrieved Jean's suitcase and they walked toward the closest elevator leading to the parking garage. For a short while, they forgot about everything else and concentrated on leaving Orlando's airport.

Heading east on I-4 toward their apartment, David and Jean debated their options.

"David, let it go. This struggle is consuming you. It's affecting your work and our relationship." Jean sighed. "Besides, we're not accomplishing anything, other than messing up our lives."

"Babe, I can't. I wish I could. I realize this is very hard on you, but I can't help it."

They were so immersed in their conversation, both failed to notice the old pickup truck just ahead of them, in the same lane, slowly drifting toward the shoulder of the express way. Its dust-covered brake light was barely visible under the bright Florida sun.

"Look out!" yelled Jean, "you're going..."

Reacting to the imminent collision, David slammed the brake pedal to the floor. The 99-Concorde's automatic braking system kept the car straight and avoided a collision with the car traveling in the next lane, toward the left. When they hit the rear end of the old truck, both airbags deployed. The seat belt restraining system stopped the movement of their bodies toward the instrument panel and David and Jean's heads were caught by the rapidly inflating airbags.

The couple and their two children traveling in the old truck hadn't seen the fast approaching red car and were totally surprised by the impact. Luckily, nobody was hurt, because the impact was slight. The truck's occupants felt a strong jolt toward the back and a moderate impact on the rear of their heads.

The driver of the old truck, Ramon Linares, quickly recovered from the collision and ran toward David's car.

"Mr., are you all right?" shouted Ramon in Spanish. "Open the door....Hurry up."

"*Paloma, andale, saca a los muchachos del camion que huele a gasolina,*" yelled Ramon to his wife, who immediately removed the children from the truck.

David and Jean were conscious but stunned, yet they reacted quickly to Ramon's screams in "Spanglish" and got out of their car immediately.

David took a good look at his car. Its front-end was severely damaged. He caught a whiff and instinctively reloaded his olfactory system for a second sniff. He didn't have any doubt; it was the unmistakable odor of radiator-coolant. In contrast the truck looked okay, only a little scar on the rear bumper—a four by four piece of wood—and a dent on the left rear fender. A classic fender bender.

"I didn't see you braking," declared David. "You can't drive that slow on the expressway; you must go at least forty miles per hour."

Ramon's facial expression was the overture of the "no-comprendo symphony." He looked one hundred percent innocent. Jean was also one hundred percent sure he was faking it.

"David, go ahead and call the police," she demanded.

"I hit him from behind...I'm sure the state trooper will give me the ticket."

"Oh...come on, don't be foolish."

Meanwhile, Paloma walked toward them, moaning and sobbing, and lamenting her bad luck.

"They didn't see us," explained Ramon in Spanish to his wife.

"They never do," retorted Paloma.

"Poor tourists...they must be in a different time," said Ramon in a tender voice.

"Holy cow! She's pregnant," exclaimed David, very surprised, almost in panic.

The situation was getting complicated. David and Jean knew very well that the real bogeyman in Central Florida was a personal injury attorney. This scourge of the legal system wasn't Gentile, Jew, Redneck, Spanish or Black. Central Florida academician (a rare specie in their own right) referred to them as the Wrongful-Death-Sue subspecies. David and Jean also knew that the members of this subspecies were always scanning their domain, that the radiator coolant scent would reach their well trained snout in the next five minutes, and that they would possibly be there, at the scene of the accident, before the police.

David and Jean looked at the truck, the pregnant woman

and each other. It was time to negotiate.

“Senor, how much money will it take to fix your truck?” asked David.

“No comprendo,” replied Ramon.

David realized it was impossible to communicate verbally with Ramon. He pulled forty-three dollars, all he had, from his wallet and waved the money in front of Ramon face.

“We need more. I need to repair the truck and take Paloma to see a Doctor. We don’t have medical insurance,” bargained Ramon in Spanish.

David looked to Jean, and asked: “Do you have any cash with you?”

“Around twenty dollars, perhaps twenty-five,” Jean frowned. “Ask him if he’ll take a check.”

Pointing at his checkbook, David asked Ramon.

“Si...si, senor,” replied Ramon, with a smile on his face.

David wrote the check for two hundred dollars and handed it to Ramon.

“Si...si. Muchas gracias,” said Ramon.

Ramon took the check and hurried his wife and children back into the truck. He was supposed to start picking ferns on Thursday, the next day, and wanted to be in Deland that night.

David managed to crank up his car. To his amazement it wasn’t overheating. It was in better shape that he expected.

His brain was urging him to forget about everything else and go immediately to a mechanic. But Jean had been gone for eight days, and his testosterone was demanding a good fuck. It was the uncontrollable urge of a twenty-nine year old male. A Jew's rational thinking is second to none among the Homo Sapiens species, and is renowned the world over as powerful and creative. But the libido of a male with his balls full of fresh sperm wins every time. David drove as fast as he could straight to their apartment.

David adored Jean, he was always in awe in front of her long, straight, slightly tanned legs. He enjoyed immensely humiliating himself and blowing her pussy up. Afterwards he would bury his head in her flat belly and just be there enjoying the Anglo-Saxon plain, and occasionally smelling the lowlands!

It was about 8:45 P.M. when they engaged again into a meaningful conversation.

"Do you actually believe that they're manipulating the media coverage of sport events?" asked Jean. "I think you're becoming a little paranoid."

"Yes, I do, and I can prove it to you." retorted David, "Let's watch the Baseball Review at 10:30 P.M."

"To late for me," declared Jean. "What's so offensive about it?"

"It's not what they say, but rather, what they don't say. Latin-American baseball players are the best ones on the league, but they consistently play down their accomplishments," replied David.

"How they do it?"

"By minimizing their on-screen time, when their performance is superb or sensational, and by showing in great detail when their performance is poor, like when they strike out. For instance, they love to show when Panduro, the big slugger, strikes out."

"It's worse in movies. They don't use Latino players, and seldom they produce films with Latino characters. It's common to see Orientals and Blacks in movies, but no Latinos," explained David.

"But why?"

"Because they want to maintain the Latin-American people in the background, out of main-stream America, with the hope that it'll delay the date when finally they'll secure the power that rightfully belongs to them," argued David.

"I don't see it," debated Jean. "I am sorry my dear, but I think you are completely wrong."

"Your attitude doesn't surprise me. We Jews know how to convince the Anglo-Saxons of almost anything. We love you, but we manipulate you."

"And so what, what that has to do with the Latinos?" asked Jean.

"A lot, it's an historical fact that we've never been able to convince them of anything. They are not against us, but they don't believe us. So, this group of business leaders is afraid of what could happen when Hispanics become the majority in this country which they believe will occur on the second half of the 21th century.

"I believe that the worst thing they can do is precisely what they're doing, ignoring and offending them. Resentment is accumulating deep in their heart, and that, my dear, is dangerous," argued David.

"Do you think Ramon knew that you were a Jew?" asked Jean.

"I don't know and I don't care," replied David, "but he referred to us as tourists."

"Tourists...are you sure?" bemusedly asked Jean.

"That is what he said."

2 The Conspiracy

Thursday, 15 April 1999

Early in the morning, David left his car in the Chrysler dealer's garage. Jean picked him up at the garage and gave him a ride to his office. Afterward, she continued on her way to the real estate office, 20 miles away, where she works as a Realtor.

Since acquiring C. Kirby enterprises from its founder's estate, the new owners had embarked on a relentless campaign to make quick money, and to bring the thinking of the American people in line with their own biased ideas. In striking contrast, the real C.K. was a compassionate man, who planted in many generations of American children tender feelings, and humanitarian ideas.

The marketing department of C. Kirby enterprises was one of the best in the nation, and it was recognized the world over as a model of efficiency. In fact, many foreign executives came to Orlando to study C.K.'s managing techniques and procedures. David was resourceful and brilliant, a first string manager with a good track record, destined to advance rapidly within the company management ranks. He had a bright future ahead of him. Actually, the only way that he could screw up and fall from the ladder of the organization, was if he rocked the boat and didn't go along with C.K.'s goals. And that was precisely what he was secretly doing!

David had his own ideas, and he didn't like at all the way that C.K.'s management conducted business. He thought that their present course of action must be blocked, and exposed for what it was—a high-tech single frequency filter that cleverly selected what ideas the American public should be exposed to, and that ridiculed and rejected anything else. Otherwise, he thought, it would bring shame and disgrace to the Jewish people. But what David didn't know was that he wasn't alone, that many other people, Jewish and Gentile alike, shared his thinking.

David reached for the in-basket and started to review his correspondence. One letter caught his attention. It was directed to the Company and passed to him for action. It was a request from "New Era," a Latino political association based in San Antonio, Texas. The letter was signed by Oreste Cardona, Executive Director. He was inquiring about the time-capsule that C.K. Enterprises was planning to bury in the year 2000 at their Florida resort. He went on to explain that "New Era" had more than one million members and that they wanted to participate in the project. Mr. Cardona requested information on how to proceed and the deadline to submit any material for inclusion in the capsule. A handwritten note, on a stick-on red tab said: "David, deny the request, but be polite, please." It was his boss' handwriting.

David first reaction was to walk into his boss office, and tell the little bastard what he thought of him and the rest of C.K.'s creeps. But, in the way there he changed his mind. He realized that the whole thing was a blessing in disguise, that it was a wonderful opportunity to put them and their ideas under the spot light, and to force the media to look into the inner works of the monster. He decided not to acknowledge the existence of the letter, to wait at least until Monday. Instead, he went straight to the copy machine and make six copies of the New Era's letter. And once back in his office he buried the letter deep into his in-basket, and put five copies inside his briefcase. He hid the remaining copy close to his computer. Then, he started to research the subject at C.K.'s private library, one of the best business libraries in the country. There, he found a lot of statistical information about Spanish population, Spanish-owned businesses, and Spanish organizations in the south-western states.

In 1999, thirty-five percent of Texas' population was Hispanic, seven million (illegals not included) strong, and rapidly increasing. New Era was organized in 1997 and since then, it had been growing by leaps and bounds. Although it had originated in San Antonio, it now had branches in every major city in Texas, and was spreading over the entire

Southwest. In fact, it had working groups in all major cities west of the Mississippi.

David had many friends in Washington. In fact, he had quick access, regardless of party, to practically any politician's staff members. All of them had requested, at one time or another, passes for C.K.'s resorts! So he called the chief of staff of the junior senator from Texas.

"Frank, old buddy, how are you doing?"

"David, my friend, glad to hear from you," replied Frank in his most charming voice, the one reserved for generous contributors and good looking chicks.

David went straight to the point, "What do you know about a Hispanic association called New Era?"

Frank's voice changed immediately to guarded and noncommittal. "Not too much, why?"

"They wrote us a letter requesting to be included in our Year 2000 Time Capsule Project," informed David. "They are based in San Antonio, right in your backyard, so you are supposed to know a lot about them."

"The grand majority of them are Democrats, and they supported us solidly in the last election," revealed Frank. "The bad news is that they are organizing a new party."

"Really, that's wonderful!" exclaimed David, "Since when?"

"I don't exactly know, but they have been collecting firms in Texas since last February."

"Do they have enough?"

"No question about it, my friend. And you better say yes in

that letter," replied Frank, "because they are a force to be reckoned with, not only in Texas, but in the entire West."

"I think you're right, but upper management is giving them a thumbs down," declared David.

"What upper management are you talking about?"

"C.K.'s upper management, who else," retorted David.

"That is incredible...are they crazy? Can you send me a copy of that letter?"

"Well...only if you treat it with the utmost confidentiality," replied David. "I'd be sticking my head out, more than I can afford. And, if its content leaks out, I'll deny everything, understood?"

"But of course, old pal, I wouldn't snitch on you," affirmed Frank. "We need to work on this matter very closely....Keep me posted."

David contacted four more "friends." He called the New York Times, the Washington Post, the Los Angeles Times, and the chief of staff of the senior senator from California.

After planting the seeds, there was nothing to do but wait. David was sure they would sprout, but he didn't what to expect.

The following Monday, Cliff Miller of Double Reel Films in Los Angeles was on the telephone talking with Max Wizenberg, his counterpart, and chief executive officer of C. Kirby Enterprises of Orlando. Cliff was a well preserved old man, who liked to challenge himself by taking on sports practiced by young and care free spirits. He did scuba diving and wind surfing. And several times he had hinted to his friends during informal conversations that he might try bungee jumping. Cliff did all that because he liked lean beef—female lean beef—and being the CEO of a film production company he had plenty of it. He had the illusion that all those cup cakes, full of delightful juices, came to him because of his young personality.

Cliff was a half-breed Jew. His mother was a first generation Jewish-American, a stern woman who never acknowledged his accomplishment, no matter how much little Cliff tried.

"We should get together and play a round of golf at your resort," proposed Cliff.

"Sure," replied Max. "What's up?"

"I'll let you know, but let's wait till we get together," explained Cliff, "Don't forget to invite your friend Joey, he is an excellent player and I enjoy his company."

"Sure, I will. What date do you have in mind?"

"How about on Tuesday, May 11," proposed Cliff.

"No good, that entire week is reserved for the media guys," replied Max. "Twice a year we invite them with all expenses, including transportation, paid."

"Son of a gun, you really know what you're doing. So, that's how you maintain that squeaky clean image."

"Sure, they and their families play, eat, and enjoy themselves at the expense of C.K. resorts.

"Besides, before they were news reporters, TV-program hosts, and disk jockeys, they were children. So our pristine image is almost indelibly engraved in their mind. In this country C.K. is the most enduring and trusted icon."

"I know, Max...when can we meet?" asked Cliff again.

"I'm free on Tuesday, May 18."

"May 18 is fine with me, but don't forget that you need to check with Joey," said Cliff. "Call me as soon as you have an answer from him."

As soon as the brief and casual conversation between the two entertainment moguls was over, Cliff's secretary went to the ladies room. She was carrying with her a tape of the entire conversation. She was an operative of the Mossad, the Jewish intelligence agency, and she had been spying on Cliff for more than six years. She placed the little tape in a pouch that she was concealing underneath her panties.

Guests of C.K. resorts can play at several golf clubs, however the "Manatee Snout" course was reserved for the exclusive use of C.K. executives and their guests. In this domain of the rich and well connected everything was free of charge with the exception of some major items in the Pro-Shop. And of course, the course was protected by the best security system that money can buy.

The small group of top executives was playing on the green of the 3rd hole. While Joey was getting ready for his putt, Cliff engaged Max in "casual" conversation, "Last month, I had a very interesting encounter with the great-granddaughter of a movie legend. She's a beautiful young lady from Orlando. Right off of the bat, she told me that the casting of our movies was very discriminatory against Hispanics."

"Is that so...what is her name?" asked Max.

"Jean Fairbanks, and I believe her boyfriend works for you."

"Not any longer," retorted Max. "Unless he has a very good excuse, and drops her like a rotten potato."

Cliff turned around and looked over his shoulder, scanning the lush surroundings of the splendid golf course. They were alone, except for the three caddies who were standing by the golf cars fifty yards away. "Don't do it. First we should find out where she comes from, what is her problem. Besides, I already put a tail on her."

"Anything so far?" asked Joey who had joined the group and was intrigued by the revelations. "Who's her boyfriend?"

Before Cliff could answer, Max gestured the caddies to go on to the next hole, that they were going to walk, rather than ride the cars.

Max was a shrewd man who trusted no one. He reached the top position of C.K. Enterprises not because he was a brilliant man or an extraordinary administrator, but because he was the great manipulator, a genius creating intrigues who kept everybody else on the defense. Systematically, shamelessly, and skillfully, he destroyed the bonds between possible contenders to his position. He would scare the living day lights of anyone of them by telling him that somebody else was plotting against him. Max wasn't a warm man, and he wasn't good looking either. He was short, his body was covered with kinky hair that grew wild in the most unexpected places. He would have been in fashion in the Stone Age, very gracious among apes and other primates. Actually, Max didn't have any excuse to be the way he was, his parents, both Jewish, were pleasant human beings.

"His name is David Szklaruk," answered Cliff, "and that's all that I know, so far."

"Son of a gun, I could not imagine him mixed up with this Mother Teresa character," declared Max. "I'm going to investigate him real close."

"Please, do that," said Joey, "but in the meantime I need to decide what to do about the Kirk Mayer and Patrick McBride situation."

"I've been watching their show. Kirk is doing an excellent job," replied Max. "We can't let McBride spoil their show with his commentaries about the excellent performance of Latin players. The 'Baseball Review' has the highest rating at that time slot. Besides, I love it when Kirk makes his trademark, attention-catching, funny noise to announce that some good old boy hit a home run."

"Me too," declared Cliff. "The 'Baseball Review' is the ideal stage for implementing our plan and influencing the preferences of millions of unsuspecting viewers. Get rid of the bastard, or promote him to a meaningless position."

Joey was the archetype of the mystical silver-fox personality. His bright lily-white hair was always well coiffured and his smile was more plastic than a credit card. He was a willing blood-sucking monster, with no remorse or regrets. As the CEO of a nationwide TV network he was the perfect complement to Cliff and Max's hold on the movie, radio, tourism, hotels, resorts, theme park, professional sport franchises and magazine industries. He knew also when to pay compliments to the powerful and rich, so, smiling, and with a matter-of-fact attitude Joey said:

"Okay...I knew I could count with you. I'll sideline him, 'til his contract is over. But I need your backing at the next BSU board meeting. I'm having strong opposition from a couple of powerful fellows who want to control Broadcasting for Sale Unlimited. Without your support I'd lose control not only of the main network, but also of the Sport and News spinoffs."

After finishing the 4th hole, the threesome of powerful executives remained on foot, and as far as they could from the caddies. Cliff and Joey were concerned that Jean noticed how the Latins were systematically ignored and put down on the network programs. They wondered if it was also obvious to the public at large. Their "project" had become risky and they were considering calling it off. Max, on the other hand, remained totally committed. In his mind he was fighting for the survival of the state of Israel. So, he reminded his two partners that with the Hispanics in power, Israel would loose the U.S.A. support, and the Islamic nations would annihilate the state of Israel. In a melodramatic voice, with overtones of indignation, Max said: "Just a couple of weeks ago we received a request from a Latino association based in Texas. They want to participate in our Time-Capsule Project!"

"And so what? What they can possible gain by participating in your project?" asked Joey.

"Don't you see it?" argued Max, "Already, they are bonding with each other. They are building the structure of a political organization."

Suddenly, Max realized that David was handling the New Era request. He became furious. The possibility of having been crossed by a young Jewish man enraged him. Max decided to punish David, to ruin him forever, and the thought of hiring a hit man to assassinate him was very alive in his agitated mind.

Reluctantly, Max agreed to wait for the report of Cliff's private investigator, before taking action himself. As a compromise, Joey suggested telling the friendly Rabbi about David's betrayal and letting him spread the word among the Jewish faithful. That alone, he argued, would be enough to discredit David beyond repair in the Jewish community. Both Cliff and Max thought that it was a good idea to let Rabbi Joseph Goldman fire the first salvo against David.

The human's brain is multilayered, onion-like, and we are linked to our most remote ancestor by the endowment embedded in these evolutionary layers. Actually, part of our brain is mammalian and part is reptilian.

Max was smart, but sometimes he behaved like a caveman. In his caveman brain he harbored aggression, terror, primitive feelings, and remote memories of animal struggle and survival. When attacked, poor Max's, reptilian mind dominates his rational mind, and he can't avoid it. So, he behaves like a snake, the only thing missing is a forked tongue. Actually, he becomes controlled by a string of very powerful commands, originating deep within his forebrain, in the dorsomedial region of the hypothalamus and in the limbic system.

3 The Leak

Wednesday, 26 May 1999

David's life was calm and steady with nothing out of the ordinary. He had been working in the promotion of the newest C.K. science fiction production, which was scheduled for release on the fourth of July. David hoped it would not turn out to be as idiotic and bombastic as the release of last fourth of July. Late that morning, however, things started to change rapidly for David when he answered the phone after it rang a couple of times.

"C. K. enterprises, this is...,"

"David, it's me. I just heard on the news channel that C.K. Enterprises rejected New Era's request," said Jean excitedly, almost breathless.

"Calm down honey...tell me, who said what?" responded David, trying to maintain his calm.

"I don't exactly know, but Jerry Bowman, the TV anchorman, was talking about last night's Lawrence Queen show. Apparently one of the guests mentioned as an example of the sad state of the racial relations in the U.S.A. that New Era, the Latino political organization, was turned down by C.K. Enterprises in their bid to participate in the Year 2000 Time Capsule Project," explained Jean.

"That is precisely what we hoped for," said David.

"And now what...what do you think will happen?" asked Jean.

"I think I'll get fired," replied David in a resigned tone of voice. "I'll see you later, honey. Right now I need to do a couple of things before I get called to the personnel office. Bye bye."

David didn't have time for anything. As soon as he hang up the phone, it rang again. He was summoned to his boss' office. There he found not only his boss, but the head of Human Resources and Max Wizenberg himself. His boss was having a bad time. His face was redder than a ripe tomato. He shouted, "The only person who had access to New Era's letter besides me was you. Why did you did it?"

David was an idealistic man, and one who would not yield in matters of principle to save his skin. He was completely committed to his cause, and was prepared to do whatever was required to promote it. Besides, he knew that nothing he could say would save his job.

He replied, "Because it was the right thing to do."

That was enough for Max, who with blazing eyes and foaming mouth rose to his feet, took a wild swing at David and screamed, "Bastard! You are an insolent son of a bitch!"

David, who was six feet tall, very athletic, and fearless jumped toward the crazed old man and wrestled him to the ground, repeatedly punching him in the chest and head. While this was going on, the personnel guy managed to open the office door and yell for security. The rest of the employees on the seventh floor could not believe their eyes, because their usually quiet office was suddenly the site of a brawl—Madison Square Garden style. They watched in horror as the security guards came into their office, guns in hand and ready to fire. They were not tender with David, they twisted his right arm against his back and whacked him on the head a couple of times. Finally, they took him out of the office, down the stairway, toward the main gate, where he was expelled like a sack of rotten potatoes.

One of C.K.'s employees called "Real Loud," a popular radio station in the Orlando area, to let them know what had happened. Orlando's local media had always been sore with C.K. enterprises, because C.K. wouldn't advertise with them. Local radio and TV stations as well as newspapers seized the opportunity to launch a massive attack against C.K. Enterprises. Real Loud went real crazy. The incident at the C.K. complex was, for them, the news of the century. They were determined to convince their audience in central Florida (or anyone who cared to listen) that C.K.'s high ranking officials were a bunch of hypocrites who for many years portrayed themselves as decent people. C.K. had always acted like people dedicated to celebrate the goodness of human nature, and to preserve the spirit and high morals of United States citizens. In reality, they were dedicated to making as much money as possible, regardless of the consequences for the country or humankind. On top of all that, they were secretly discriminating against millions of Latin American citizens.

The news, now a scandal with national and international implications, was given front page coverage in most of the leading newspaper of the country. National TV channels covered it in prime time, and analyzed it from all angles and perspectives.

Under the barrage of insults and negative comments, and pressured by powerful advertisers, C.K. enterprises apologized to New Era, and publicly announced that they were welcome to participate in the Year 2000 Time Capsule Project.

David remained fired, but it was a moral victory for him. He was delighted when he received the support and encouragement of many progressive Jewish organizations based in New York and other large cities around the country.

In contrast, Max never apologized. He trusted his caveman instinct and hid as well as he could. He was determined to keep his original plans alive, no matter what. But first he wanted to take care of David, and he intended to do it in the first opportunity, as soon as the shock waves of the scandal subsided.

On Memorial Day, Joey called Cliff on the hot line—a telephone which was separate and independent from the rest of Double Reel Films' telephone system, and which was answered directly by Cliff Miller.

"Cliff...this is Joey. I just received a call from the Israeli ambassador."

"Really...what did he say?"

"This is hard to believe, but he wants to have a meeting with you, me, and Max," replied Joey, "Isn't that strange?"

"Indeed, my friend," concurred Cliff, "Did he say when he wants to have the meeting?"

"As soon as possible, sometime this week," answered Joey, "and he sounded crisp and demanding...as if he knew what was going on."

"That's weird...amazing, how could he?" affirmed Cliff in disbelief. "We need to get in touch with Max immediately and inform him."

"I'll take care of that," said Joey. "Perhaps we could all talk in a conference call."

"Bad idea," retorted Cliff, "and be prepared because our friend might go ballistic when he learns about this."

"I know, but that is an offer that we can't refuse. If his excellency wants a meeting, he's going to get one. "

The meeting was set for Friday at the embassy of Israel in Washington, D.C. The three media moguls rose to their feet when the ambassador came into the office. He said, "Good morning gentlemen."

"Good morning sir," the visitors replied in unison.

"Please, sit down."

In comparison with his guests' private offices, the ambassador's office was small and simply decorated. Nevertheless, the presence of his excellency, the prestige of the office, and the legendary reputation of Israel evoked on the Jewish-Americans an overwhelming feeling of respect toward the place and the man across the heavy wooden desk. The ambassador's demeanor was somber, and he didn't care to initiate any friendly small talk before getting to the subject of the meeting.

"We know all about your plan to keep the Hispanic-Americans out of the political mainstream in America," declared the Ambassador, "and we know that you are doing it with the intention of helping Israel."

The Jewish executives were surprised to hear the Ambassador's blunt statement; they exchanged gazes of distress. They realized that they had been caught in the act, but didn't know how and when.

Joey managed to ask, "How do you know? Who told you?"

The ambassador reclined on his swivel chair and looking directly into the old fox's eyes retorted, "Sir, we have the best intelligence agency in the world."

"Were they spying on us?" asked Cliff.

"They were collecting information," replied the Ambassador, "You cannot work on our behalf without our involvement. We must know what is going on in matters affecting the state of Israel."

"Who do you think you are?" protested Max, "You can't intimidate me. I have very powerful friends both in the government and in the opposition party in Israel, and I intend to let them know what you just said. You can't treat us this way! We have contributed millions of dollars to Israel....I'm going to make sure that you are punished for this."

Cliff realized that things were getting out of hand, so before the ambassador could reply to Max's outburst, he intervened and said: "Mr. Ambassador, we are disappointed because we have invested a lot of our money and time trying to protect our mother land from a terrible situation in a not distant future. Israel cannot survive without the active support of the United State Government."

"That is precisely the point, but there are things that you can't change. We must face our destiny without creating more rancor and mortal enemies. We estimate that before the 21st century is over, Latin-Americans will assume control of this country, and there is nothing you can do about it. So we don't want to upset them by intervening in the country's politics against their interests. If you really want to help the state of Israel, the best thing you can do is to be good American citizens. You must abandon your wicked campaign against Latin-American role models and leaders. If you don't, we will make sure that you are prosecuted. We can provide the FBI with enough evidence to keep you in jail for the rest of your lives. Something else, Mr.Wizenberg you are nothing but a despicable black-mailer. We demand that you resign your position with C. Kirby Enterprises," declared the Ambassador.

Max detonated. He spat on the ambassador's face and screamed, "Sephardic! You are a disgusting Ladino-speaking Sephardic. And a shit-smelling Marrano....queer!"

The Ambassador had had enough of Max, so he pressed the

panic button. Seconds later, embassy security guards grabbed Max and took him away. He was still kicking and screaming when he was thrown out of the embassy security detachment black car onto a grassy section of Rock Creek Park.

Initially, Murphy's law was a joke, a sarcastic declaration that talented engineering students often quoted. Now it had taken a life of its own. It says: if something can go wrong, it probably will.

Max was bitter that he was forced to resign as Chief Executive Officer of C. Kirby Enterprises. Even his old buddies, Joey and Cliff, had turned against him. Max blamed David for his demise and he was determined to carry out a plan to assassinate him. He still had the telephone number of a Sicilian hit man that he used to get rid off the Chairman of the Board of Marivel Corporation, when years ago C.K. Enterprises was in the process of acquiring Marivel Corporation. But he was afraid to call him from the U.S.A. Written communication was also out of the question. So on the sixth of July, 1999, he took TWA flight 390 out of Orlando, and in Kennedy Airport, New York, he boarded TWA flight 840 to Rome, Italy. He arrived there at 8:40 in the morning of July 7.

Max had been to Italy many times before, but always as an executive of C. K. Enterprises. As such, there was always an entourage of employees and business associates attending to all the details and minor inconveniences that people usually experience on their arrival to a foreign country. The limousine was always waiting for him. But now he was on his own. He despised the stupidity of the Italians and the gross inefficiencies that he encountered at the airport. For him it was unthinkable to have the rental-car counters on the fourth floor of the parking garage across the road. Once he crossed the road he could not find the entrance to the parking facility, so he turned to a bystander who was casually leaning against a street lamppost. In English he asked the stranger, "Sir, can you tell me where the entrance to this building is?"

"I don't understand, senor," replied the bystander in Spanish.

Max liked to spend his vacations in Mexico more than anywhere else. He had learned enough Spanish to get by in Mexico and many other Latin American countries.

"Are you Mexican?" asked Max in Spanish. "What are you doing here?"

"A hundred percent Mexican," responded the bystander, "I came to pick grapes in southern Italy."

"I was unaware that you Mexicans came all the way to Italy to pick grapes." said Max. "Where is Europcar, the rental car company?"

"In the fourth floor," answered the bystander. "Do you see that plastic roof?"

"Yes."

"Go in there, take the moving sidewalk and follow the sign," explained the bystander.

"Okay, but where is the elevator to get to the fourth floor?" asked Max.

"Don't worry, you will find it at the end of the run," affirmed the bystander.

Max was impressed by the efficiency of the friendly Mexican. The likable fellow treated him with respect and courtesy.

"Senor, what is your name?" shouted Max as he walked toward the covered walkway.

"Ramon Linares," yelled the bystander.

After the long transatlantic flight, Max hoped he could relax while cruising on the Autostrada on his way to Naples; however, driving in Italy is very competitive to say the least, and especially so on the expressways. Autostrada A1 was a nightmare for him. Regardless of how fast he drove the medium size Fiat, he was forced out of his lane by larger cars that demanded the right of way.

The view from Max's room at the Hotel Paradiso in Naples was splendid. He could see the entire bay and Mount Vesuvius. Finally, he was able to relax and have some time to pull his thoughts together. He took a bottle of "Lacryma Christi del Vesuvio," an exquisite local white wine, from the bar and sat down to enjoy both the view and the wine. Before finishing the glass of wine he reached for the telephone and called his contact in Sicily.

"Do you speak English?"

"Non capisco," replied the man who answered the telephone.

Max tried then to speak in Italian.

"Please, I like to speak with Gennaro," said Max in broken Italian.

"Gennaro is dead."

For an instant Max thought of dropping the whole thing right there, but Max was not a quitter.

"I need someone for a job."

"Who are you and where are you?" asked the man.

"Hotel Paradiso in Naples, room 508," replied Max.

"I need your name."

"Max," reluctantly replied Max.

"Max what?" persisted the man.

"Morgan...Max Morgan."

"We'll call you," declared the man before hanging up the phone.

Max waited at the Paradiso for the rest of the day. The next day, having nothing else to do, he decided to drive from Sorrento to Amalfi on Corniche Road which runs high over the blue waters of the "Golfo di Salerno." Corniche Road is a two narrow laned "highway" that seemed to have been carved out of an infinite number of cliffs. In this part of Southern Italy an entire ridge of mountains abruptly end as they plunge into the ocean.

The drive had a healing effect on Max's mind. Taking the risky curves at high speed and watching the ocean blue waters way down there, more than a thousand feet below, induced in him a sense of well being. It was risky but delightful. He stopped in the village of Positano and contemplated the myriad of little houses clinging precariously to hills and mountains. Upon returning to the hotel, Max felt goodness in his heart. He felt reborn, with a bright future ahead of him.

The phone rang while Max was taking a shower. Nevertheless, he answered the call before the fourth ring.

"Max Wizenberg?" inquired the same man he spoke to before.

"Yes."

"We want to see you tonight at eight o'clock."

"Where?"

"Ristorante Buca di Greco," replied the man, "It's on Corniche Road, past Positano."

"I just came from there," affirmed Max. "It's too far away, I don't believe I can be there on time. It is almost six o'clock now."

"No problem, he'll wait for you," said the man.

"Who is he?" asked Max.

"Gennaro's replacement," replied the man before hanging up the phone.

It was ten past eight when Max arrived at the restaurant. Buca di Greco was perched on a ridge high above the ocean, with its single white structure surrounded by dripping flowers. It was a bewitching place, glimmering in the night like a genuine gem. It seemed unreal, almost heavenly.

The host at the entrance was elegantly attired and was doing his best to give the impression that Boca di Greco was a high-class restaurant, where every effort was made to please their refined clientele. Max was taken to a table with a dazzling view of the sea below and the sky above.

A middle-aged man was seated at the table, who said, “Please, sit down.”

“I’m Max,” said Max while shaking hands with the man.

“Lorenzo Burgio,” replied the man.

Lorenzo was a man of stocky medium height and bushy dark hair. His forehead was narrow and served as the launch pad for a heavy-duty nose.

Both men focused their attention on the menu that the waiter handed to them. After ordering their meals, Lorenzo told the waiter, “bring me a bottle of the best local white wine.”

“Be sure it’s made with ‘Coda di Volpe’ grapes,” instructed Max. “I know that you grow them here, on the slopes of Mount Vesuvius.”

“It surprises me that you are so well acquainted with the wines of this region,” said Lorenzo.

“I’m from California...I took a couple of wine making courses in college,” replied Max. “So, I’m not your typical American, familiar only with Chianti.”

“You can’t be like a typical American.”

“Why not?”

“You are Jewish, aren’t you?”

Max wasn’t expecting that kind of remark, and in southern Italy, didn’t know how to react to it. Back in the states it would had been very offensive. Max managed to put a lid on his temper and changed the subject of the conversation. “How did you find out what my real name was?”

“You left your passport at the front desk of the hotel,” replied Lorenzo. “We know everything about you, Mr. Wizenberg. So, don’t lie to me anymore, it is dangerous.”

“I’m traveling incognito, and everything we agree to must be totally confidential and secret,” declared Max. “This must be our first and last meeting.”

“Of course, we understand your position. We are expert in this business, and we too have a reputation to maintain. So what can we do for you?”

Lorenzo was looking straight in Max eyes, he was confident and challenging.

“I want to put out a contract,” said Max.

“A contract for what?”

Max drank the wine that was left in his glass, uttered a sound of approval, and refilled the glass.

“Excellent wine,” affirmed Max. “I want to eliminate some-one.”

“And that someone is...” persisted Lorenzo.

“David...David Szklaruk,” responded Max. “He lives in Orlando, Florida. He betrayed me....he is a renegade...a traitor who used to work for me.”

Max was on a roll. He finished his second glass of wine and ordered a new bottle.

“Can you do it? How much do you want?”

“Is he a politician, a leader of the community, a celebrity, or connected to the police in some fashion?” inquired Lorenzo.

“No way...he is an insignificant punk,” retorted Max.

“In that case, It will cost you a hundred and fifty thousand dollars,” affirmed Lorenzo in business like fashion.

“Are you kidding?” asked Max rhetorically. He was ready to start bargaining.

Lorenzo knew that Max was in a precarious position, that

he didn't have any other choice. So nonchalantly he declared, "Mr. Wizenberg...you are dealing with the headquarters of the Mafia. That is our final price, take it or leave it."

Max wiped off his mouth with the back of his hand. He was nervous, because a big struggle was going on inside his mind. On one hand, he felt the urge to reject Lorenzo's demand and leave, on the other he hated to even think that David could go unpunished—the thought of a victorious David was not acceptable to him. Finally, his schizophrenic mind arrived at a decision.

"Okay, I'll pay a half now, and the other half when the job is completed."

"No, we don't work that way. We want the whole amount now."

"I don't have that kind of money with me."

"Don't lie to me...I bet it is in the trunk of your car."

"How do you know?" asked Max.

"Where else it could be? Not in a bank...not in the hotel safe, and of course not in your room."

Max felt trapped, ambushed by the Mob. His ears became tomato-red.

"I'm a business man, with excellent credit. Where I come from everybody knows that I paid my debts on time. But you don't trust me, do you?"

"No, I don't," calmly replied Lorenzo. "But don't freak out on me...this way is much better. You wouldn't need to contact us anymore. Our hit-man will take care of David, and the beautiful part is that you don't know who is he, and he doesn't know you either. The transaction will be completed, and shortly after, David will be dead, guaranteed."

Lorenzo's pitch was very convincing. His experience in these matters became obvious to Max, and he liked that.

"Okay, you got a deal," said Max.

"I am glad you made the right decision," stated Lorenzo, "but I need David's address or phone number."

"He lives in Lake Breeze Apartments in Winter Park, apartment 329," replied Max.

"Does he lives alone?"

"No, he lives with his girl-friend," replied Max. "Her name is Jean Fairbanks."

"Do you want to hit her also?" inquired Lorenzo.

"No...but it would be nice," responded Max, "because she might have been the instigator, the real culprit. But I don't know that for sure."

Everything was settled, so after they finished dinner and Lorenzo paid the bill, they proceeded to the tiny parking lot across the highway from the restaurant. Max went directly to his car, opened the trunk and withdrew an old, brown brief case.

"Is this place secure?" asked Max.

"Oh yeah...don't worry we are safe."

"I have here two hundred thousand dollars," disclosed Max. "I'm going to take out five bundles of ten thousand each. You can take the rest."

"Listen, for those five bundles, we will take care of Jean also," proposed Lorenzo. "how does that sound to you?"

"You know what, that is a good idea," replied Max smiling. "Let's do it, take the whole thing."

"Don't worry Mr.Wizenberg, we will take care of them for you," said Lorenzo. "Have a safe return trip."

Max never noticed the tail that Lorenzo put on him on his way over, and that now was following him on his way back. He was feeling good, because he had accomplished what he came to Italy for. He thought that he could now return to a normal life, and enjoy the money he had stockpiled in his long career. He was a very wealthy man. The feeling of well being was blocking off everything else. He was enjoying immensely the action of taking the countless curves of Corniche Road while listening to an old Mexican song on the radio. The song that mysteriously was being played on all the frequencies of his car radio. Helped by the wine and the delicious meal the euphoric feelings were transformed into an uncontrollable urge for sleeping. Finally, he surrendered and felt sleep.

His car plunged into the abyss and disappeared in the deep waters of the dark ocean. It was a happy death, at least that was what the two gangsters following him reported to Lorenzo.

It was a golden opportunity for Lorenzo, who "canceled" the contract and kept the money. Ironic indeed, that David and Jean were spared of a sure death by the good feelings that overcame Max.

4 New Era

Wednesday, 9 June 1999.

In the Royal Mayan Room on the first floor of the Holiday Inn on East San Antonio, Texas, Oreste Cardona was having a hard time bringing to order the meeting. "Ladies and gentlemen, members of the National Executive Committee, sit down please," repetitively announced Oreste in Spanish.

Finally, the eighteen attendees sat around several tables arranged to form a U-shaped setting place, and the meeting started. Daniel Vargas, the Secretary of the National Executive Committee, walked the members throughout the silly initial procedural steps. After that cumbersome part was out of the way, Oreste addressed the group.

"I want to congratulate the Texas delegates for a job well done. The signature collection drive in Texas has been completed. We collected more than twice the number of signatures required to get into the year 2000 election ballot in Texas.

"The purpose of this meeting is to discuss the events generated by our request to participate in C.K. Enterprises, year 2000 Time Capsule Project. Here is a summary of those events.

"On April 8th of this year we wrote a letter to C.K. requesting our participation on the Year 2000 Time Capsule Project.

"On May 25th, in the Lawrence Queen show, it was revealed that C.K. denied our request.

"In the next couple of days, the news received extensive coverage by the media.

"On Friday, May 28th, Edward Phillips III, C.K. president for corporate affairs held a news conference, in which he apologized to New Era and welcomed our participation.

"On June 6th, in the Sunday Edition of the Washington Post, Greg Jones reported in his column—The Sleazy Shadow—about an incident in the Israeli embassy in which Max Wizenberg, the deposed CEO of C. Kirby enterprises, was forcefully expelled from the embassy, and released in an isolated area of Rock Creek Park.

"We received, from all over the country, thousand of letters, faxes, and phone calls. They came from all segments of the population, Latino and non-Latino, and they all supported our cause and expressed anger against C.K.

"The incident is also all over the Internet," said Mireya Hernandez, the delegate from New York city, "and the response is overwhelmingly in our favor."

Mireya's simple comment broke the ice, and the other attendees began to voice their opinions.

"The Orlando Sentinel published a description of the incident," declared Victor Machado, the delegate from Central Florida. "They interviewed many employees of C.K."

"Really...what did the article say?" asked Oreste.

"That David Szklaruk, one of the employees, was called into his boss' office, where he encountered not only his boss, but the chief of the personnel department, and Max Wizenberg, the CEO. They were arguing very loudly when suddenly a fist fight erupted between David and the CEO. The chief of the personnel department summarily fired David on the spot, as C.K. security guards grabbed and expelled him from the office complex," Replied Victor.

"What was the fight all about?" inquired Oreste.

"The article isn't clear about this, but it appears that David was the guy that leaked to the press the position taken by C.K. upper management, before they could actually reject our request," replied Victor.

"Is he Jewish?" asked Mireya.

"Who?"

"David."

"Yes," replied Victor.

"I have a gut feeling that there is a lot more to this incident, and that what we already know is only the tip of the iceberg," declared Sergio Estrada, one of the delegates from California.

"Some Jewish organizations of the New York metropolitan area are very concerned with the power acquired by Hispanics in recent years, and what it could do to the American-Jewish relations. In fact, we know that some of them are trying to slow down our progress. They target our leaders and role models, whether they are politician, artists, or baseball players, and systematically try to diminish their accomplishment in the eyes of the general public. These Jewish organizations block, ridicule or tame the development of our most brilliant people," declared Mireya.

"In Hollywood, they have been doing the same thing for many years. Not only to Hispanics, but to anyone else that could represent a challenge to their power," affirmed Sergio. "They tried to slow down the career of many famous and not so famous people, like Orson Welles, Dean Martin, James Garner, Anthony Quinn, Raoul Julia. And it's a well known 'secret' that anyone who performed in the Lawrence Welk Show didn't have a chance in Hollywood."

"Do you remember how that obnoxious sports announcer, what was his name?...whatever...tormented Muhammad Ali, and then tried to pass himself as a good friend and sympathizer of the great champion," said Francisco Pedrosa, the delegate from Chicago. "And Jesse Jackson has endured a relentless campaign to discredit him in the eyes of the American public."

"And you can dance like Fred Astaire, look like Gary Grant, have Richard Burton flair, and act like Edward G. Robinson. But if you don't suck the Jewish dick you won't have a chance to win an Oscar," added Sergio.

"That isn't true. Oscar winners are selected by the five thousand members of the Academy of Motion Pictures," argued Pancho Lubian.

"Where are you from?" Asked Sergio

"From Miami."

"No wonder."

"You're talking nonsense, and you know it," declared Pancho.

"All these happened because Robert Kennedy attacked and crippled most of the Mafia families across the country. Free of this natural counterbalance the Jewish expanded without limit in New York, Hollywood, and Las Vegas," argued Ernesto Davila, the delegate from New Mexico.

"The Anglos have always being afraid of the Jewish retaliation. This was obvious in June, 1967, when the Israelis attacked in international waters the USS Liberty, an intelligence-gathering ship of the U.S. Navy. For more than two hours the Jewish air force and navy bombed and torpedoed the USS Liberty. Without mercy, the perpetrators of the cowardly attack strafed and destroyed the American's lifeboats before they could be deployed. The thirty four American sailors that lost their life and the 179 who were wounded could not imaging that an allied nation would carry out such a treacherous attack. But, perhaps more shameful was the lack of reaction of the U.S. Government," revealed Mireya.

It was a free-for-all, a shameful regurgitation of anti-Semitic gossip silently accumulated throughout years of intense resentment. Never before in this country had a group of Hispanic people dared to bash and discredit the Jewish race without consideration to the consequences. The anti-Semitic orgy continued unabated for several more minutes and it degenerated into ugly jokes about the non-existence of Jewish restaurants and the rocking motion in front of the Wailing Wall.

Unexpectedly someone began to shout. The angry voice was coming from the rear of the room, from somewhere near the entrance.

"Racists!...racist! You are a despicable bunch of racists!" shouted the heckler in Spanish.

The delegates were totally surprised, it never occurred to them that they could be accused of being racists. More than a minute passed before Oreste could respond to the verbal attack of the heckler. Finally, he yelled back to him in Spanish: "Who the hell are you?"

"Ramon Linares."

"You don't belong here," declared Oreste.

"Thank you, sir, I'm glad I don't."

"Well in that case you must leave immediately."

"Not before you heard me."

"I don't need to listen to you," proclaimed Oreste. "Would somebody, please, call the hotel security."

"If you don't let me speak, I'll tell the press about your anti-Semitic remarks," announced Ramon.

"Oreste, let him speak. Let's see what he has to say," interjected Victor Machado.

Reluctantly, Oreste agreed with Victor's proposal. He said: "Okay, you have the floor for five minutes."

Ramon did not come forward to the conference table, he stayed close to the door. He declared: "I also think that we

Latinos must organize a new political party, a party to promote the interests of the Hispanic Nation. And I believe that New Era could be such a party."

Ramon was interrupted by Ernesto Davila, who asked, "Where are you from?"

"From El Paso. I was born right here, in Texas."

"How come we don't know you?" persisted Ernesto. "You are very articulate...you speak like a seasoned politician or a preacher."

"Are you going to let me speak or what?" retorted Ramon. "As I was saying...New Era could be the party of the future, the largest political party in this nation by the end of the 21th century. But to achieve that status, we must free ourselves of racial prejudices, and judging for what I heard hear today, that is a monumental task. You were indiscriminately attacking the Jewish people without taking in consideration that David, a Jewish man, was the one that exposed the prejudiced actions of C. Kirby Enterprises. David risked everything: his job, the relationship with his girlfriend, and his life. And he did that without asking for any kind of reward. It was a noble act, more than any of you will do for people of another race. You are Catholic, aren't you? Well Jesus Christ was Jewish, and so was his mother, the Virgin Mary."

"Wait a minute, who said that David's life was in jeopardy?" asked Mireya.

"I read that in the New York Times," replied Ramon, "Apparently, Max Wizenberg went to Italy to put a contract on David's life with the Sicilian Mafia. Ironically, Max died in a car accident before he could close the deal."

"It's amazing how well informed you are," declared Mireya, "I think you're an FBI agent, there is not any other logical explanation."

Mireya's declaration must had stimulated a highly sensitive area in the other delegates' mind, because collectively and simultaneously they became enraged. The thought of being the target of an FBI sting operation teed-off a wacky response. Like kamikaze bees they swarmed toward Ramon and grabbed him. Then, before expelling him from the room, they insulted him and his ancestors in both languages, Spanish and English.

The high-fives were still flying when Oreste Cardona called for a premature lunch-break: "Gentlemen, it's lunch time! We'll reconvene at twelve thirty."

During lunch the main topic of conversation among delegates was Ramon the "renegade." So, Oreste started the afternoon session discussing Ramon's allegations, instead of following his original schedule.

"I know you feel offended by Ramon's accusations, and rightfully so, because we Latinos are the least racist of all the ethnic groups making up this society. A Latino or Hispanic person could be of practically any race or mix of races, our identity is based on a multitude of characteristics, like language, country of origin, Spanish heritage, and surname. A Latino could be white and of European extraction, could be Black, could be Amerindian, or could be of Asiatic extraction. This business about our relationship with the Jewish people is the wrong business for us, there are many other issues that are more important to us, but now that Ramon opened this ugly can of worms, we must deal with it.

"Jews are few in number, relatively speaking, but they command great power because they have money, they are smart and well organized, and they know how to disseminate and sell their ideas.

"These marketing geniuses has left the American public with two choices: either accept the Jew's point of view or you would be disgraced and repudiated by everybody else. So, the Jewish perspective has become sacred, always in the front page, yet it cannot be exposed or attacked. In fact, many Americans believe it is impolite to talk about Christmas without mentioning in the same sentence the Jewish Hanukkah. We have a lot to learn from them and they aren't our enemies. So, it's in our best interest to cultivate their friendship and emulate them.

"By the end of the 21th century or perhaps at the beginning of the 22nd, Hispanics will be the largest ethnic group in this country, but not by much. The Anglo-Saxons and Blacks ethnic groups will be almost as large. In the mean time, we must organize ourselves, and reduce to a minimum the infighting among the different nationalities within our Hispanic group. We must present to the rest of this country a united Latino front. Then and only then, we could claim the power that rightfully belongs to us. There are some Anglo politicians that want to dismember the Hispanic community. Their biased propaganda machinery is intent in creating a new ethnic classification. They want to label us as multiracial. In fact, this classification is not applicable, because all the ethnic groups in this country are multiracial. For instance, a white person could be of Anglo, German, Polish, Italian, Iris, Slavic, Sweden, Croatian, Finish, Dutch, etc. stock.

"Regarding our friend, David Szklaruk, I think that we must thank him for his generosity and for the gutsy work he did in our behalf.

"Why we don't hire David to be our Marketing Manager?" interrupted Ernesto Davila. "He must be a public relations wizard."

"I second that motion," stated Mireya.

"Are the members of the National Executive Committee in favor of hiring David?" asked Oreste.

"Yes," responded all the delegates, in unison.

"Okay...Victor, he's your man. He lives right there in Orlando, so you're the logical selection to contact and hire him," stated Oreste. "You can offer him up to one hundred twenty thousand dollars per year. But he'll need to move to San Antonio."

Oreste was glad that finally David's incident was taken care of and he could proceed with the other items in his agenda. He announced: "We need to decide what is going to be our contribution to the year 2000 Time Capsule project."

"That sound very good, but who is going to find out what happened in the Israeli embassy?" asked Pancho Lubian, the delegate from Miami.

"On that item, I think that it's best to wait for David. He should be able to handle it better that any of us," replied Oreste.

Part Two - 2077

5 The Texas Connection

Wednesday, 12 May 2077

"What's up, amigo?" I said watching my friend's face on the telephone monitor.

"You better ask your computer," replied Rafi Fuentes. "The latest poll shows we're losing big."

"How is that?"

"The Texas independence drive was favored by sixty-nine percent of the respondents. We are far behind. Only twenty percent of the respondents want to stay in the union. Eight percent want to join Mexico. The remaining three percent isn't sure," Rafi said.

"That's terrible. We're going to get chewed out by the members of New Era's National Executive Committee. Especially by Senator Santamarina."

"You got that one right, man. I'm glad you'll do the explaining and not me," declared Rafi.

"I'll make sure you get your fair share of blame, buddy."

"At what time are we leaving today?" Rafi asked.

"I'd like to catch the 5:45 shuttle. I promised my wife I'd take her to the old River Walk tonight. I need to be in San Antonio around 6 o'clock."

"If we hurry, we can make it," said Rafi. "It's now 4:25 so we have an hour and twenty minutes to reach Union City."

"I hope you're right. But don't forget that we need to go through the Lincoln Tunnel and that, my friend, is a real bottle neck. I'll see you at the parking garage in five minutes."

I didn't have to commute daily from San Antonio to New York City. I had a flexible work schedule that allowed me to work from home; after all, I was the boss. Usually, I stayed in New York on Monday and Tuesday nights and returned home on Wednesdays, after work. Most of the time I stayed in San Antonio for the rest of the week. Occasionally, however, I traveled somewhere else.

The first half of the second week of May 2077 was a hectic one for me. I was looking forward to the usual midweek break and wanted to leave New York as soon as possible. Paradoxically, it would take me four times longer to go from Manhattan to Union City, only forty miles away, than to travel 1,900 miles from Union City to San Antonio.

In the second half of the 21th century, airplanes could fly very low at maximum speed. They were safe and easy to fly. Navigation was entirely computer controlled. However, they weren't the fastest mode of transportation. Air friction and drag were still unsurmountable problems.

The transcontinental shuttle traveled at 6,200 miles per

hour, inside plastic tubes, in which a vacuum had been created to minimize friction and drag. The tubes were laid across the continent, above, on, or underground, as part of the Extremely Fast Long Range Transportation System, developed in the 2040's by the Federal Government. Each coach was magnetically levitated and propelled by linear electric motors. The Americans of the third millennium found themselves in a similar situation to their 19th century counterparts, who could travel by train across the continent in four days, but once they reached their destination found themselves depending on horse-drawn transportation.

Before leaving the office I took a quick look at my desk and verified I hadn't forgotten anything. I put on my ten gallon hat and walked out to the hall. The first down-going elevator car didn't stop, apparently full. Nothing strange at quitting time. Finally, after a few anxious seconds, I was going down to the upper level of the parking garage, where I had left my car early in the morning.

Someone riding with me shouted, “Hey, Tito! When are you going to trade your ten-gallon hat for the Mexican sombrero?”

I recognized the voice of Sam Stielberg.

“Sam, if you keep that up, you're going to find yourself alone in somebody else's land,” I said, “and you know what I mean.”

“Okay, amigo, just checking, but you never answered my question.”

I turned around and stared down into his eyeballs. “I don't need to answer your questions. Comprende, amigo?”

His facial expression darkened. He smiled nervously. He didn't want to mess around with me. He was saved by the bell. The sound of the elevator bell returned color to his face.

Rafi was already there, standing by my car.

"Let's go."

"What is the matter man? You look upset," affirmed Rafi.

"No big deal. On my way down I've the misfortune of riding with Sam."

"What Sam?"

"You know the Jerk of the 62nd floor, the one that works for C.K. Enterprises."

"Oh...man. Don't let him upset you," declared Rafi. "He is a sarcastic asshole, looking for attention and security."

"Yes, but why me?"

"Because, you represent the Latinos, the largest ethnic group in this country."

I started the car and drove out to Union City, I consistently avoided public transportation because it wasn't safe and it was always very crowded at rush-time.

"Perhaps we can save some time if we take the Holland Tunnel," said Rafi, "or the Mario Cuomo Tunnel."

"No way, Jose! I tried both routes, either one would take longer."

Propelled by its fifty horse-power, frequency controlled, AC motor, my electric car was zipping along, as fast as it could be expected on a Wednesday at 5:10 P.M. When the well modulated voice of the Message Center in the instrument panel became operational, it brought us a prerecorded message that was out of sync with our conversation, yet it got our attention immediately.

"Recharge the power-pak now! You have 30 more minutes of running-time before the power runs out." stated the invisible messenger.

"Shit....we don't have time. I think we can make it to the shuttle station," I said.

"When was the last time that you recharged the power-pack?" Rafi asked.

"About five months ago. This new model lasts about 5,000 miles."

"Yes, I heard about it. How does it work?" asked Rafi.

I had a Master's Degree in nuclear physics from the University of Texas at Austin, and worked for three years at the nearby particle accelerator. So I was glad that I had a chance to brief Rafi—a graduate from the Harvard Law school, and a consummate know it all—in the operation of the nuclear power-pack.

"It's a new shield made of a gel in plasma state which absorbs practically all the stray Beta particles. So, they can use a larger radioactive core.

"In the old chemically-activated batteries, acid diluted in water provided the ions to create an electric current. In nuclear power-packs, beta particles emitted by the radioactive atomic nuclei are the ones that produce the electromotive force that drives the car's electric motor."

"Any byproduct from the decay of the radioactive material?" he asked.

"A whole bunch of neutrinos," I replied. "Nothing can stop them, but fortunately they are harmless."

I lined up my car in one of the six in-lanes of the shuttle station long-term parking facility. Before I could gain access to the parking lot, a laser-beam reader decoded the information contained in the credit-plate located on the side of my car. I read the in-time, now displayed in the upper console of my car—it was 5:30 P.M., 12 May 2077.

I was lucky, I found a parking space in less than two minutes. Rafi wasn't surprised, however, because we commuted twice a week and we were very familiar with the parking facility.

"We have thirteen minutes to reach the departing gate," Rafi said, as we walked briskly along the people mover leading to the southwest region wharf which handles the South Western states traffic.

"We need to find out the number of the gate," I said.

"It's gate... 26...lower-level pier," replied Rafi after looking toward a giant monitor hanging from the roof.

Finally, we boarded the transcontinental shuttle. We walked along the center aisle up to the last car where we found a couple of empty seats, next to each other. All shuttle seats were individually mounted and the separation between them was such that they could be laid out flat without touching each other.

I watched the shuttle trip's instructions in the seat's TV monitor.

Attention! The shuttle engine cannot start until all passengers have complied with the trip's instructions. You must follow the captain's commands as they are displayed in the monitor.

Strap your legs now!

Recline your seat all the way back.

Close and latch your seat's cover!

Thank you.

Don't open your seat's cover during the trip.The air pressure inside the shuttle's cabin is very low.

You will feel a minor jolt when the shuttle is levitated inside the evacuated plastic tubes.

You will feel a gentle push for the first and the last three minutes of the trip, while the shuttle accelerates or brakes at fifty feet per second every second.

The shuttle will reach its cruising speed of 6,200 miles per hour in three minutes. It will maintain that speed for 12.6 minutes.

The shuttle will decelerate for three minutes, before coming to a complete stop.

Total travel time to San Antonio, 18.6 minutes.

Once the shuttle reached its cruising speed, I called Rafi over the shuttle's internal communication system.

"I'm sick and tired of the idiotic trip's instructions. Remind me to write a letter to the Shuttle Authority."

"I'm trying to get a little siesta here....Mr. Big Shot," replied Rafi. "Would you mind?"

"No."

6 The Accident

Wednesday, 12 May 2077

We arrived in San Antonio at 4:05 P.M. and walked toward the exit where my wife Marta, usually waits for me. I spotted her car and told Rafi, "There she is."

"Yeah, I see her too."

We reached her car in a few more steps.

"Have you been waiting long, dear?"

"No, but hurry and get in. Something terrible's happened," she shouted.

"What's wrong?" I asked while getting into the car. Rafi hopped into the back seat.

"Tony just got killed," she replied while pulling out of the parking space.

"Our neighbor's son?" I asked. "When? What happened?"

"Earlier in the afternoon, the Sanchez and Tony went to Lake Calaveras with their new jet-boat. Miguel wanted to teach little Tony how to operate the boat. They were approaching the main dock by the launching ramp when a drunken idiot, driving a large speed-boat at full speed rammed their boat on the starboard side."

"That's awful! Was anyone else hurt?"

"Both Xiomara and Miguel were badly injured, but they are expected to survive."

Rafi asked, "Do I know them?"

"You played dominoes with them about two weeks ago," I said. "Xiomara was your partner. Remember?"

"Oh, yeah—poor kid! He was such a nice little guy, so well behaved. I can't believe that he's dead."

Fifteen minutes later, we dropped Rafi off at his building, and in three more minutes, we drove into the parking garage of our building complex three miles down the road.

The Golden Tortilla—the newest residential complex in San Antonio—is a dome enclosed community free of ultraviolet radiation, dust, and rain, with a delightful controlled environment. There are twelve 22-floor residential buildings laid out so that they also serve as pillars to support the tinted plastic dome. The Golden Tortilla's center is a huge atrium, that serves as hub and focus of the community, and contains recreational areas, restaurants, and all kinds of shops and boutiques.

Instead of going out to dinner, Marta and I spent Wednesday evening at the hospital with Xiomara and Miguel. A heartrending time—because Tony had been just ten years old and was their only son. Miguel and Xiomara immigrated to this country twelve years ago from Colombia. I felt great compassion for Miguel because I knew that he'd been very close to his brilliant son. I knew they were more to each other than father and son. They'd been inseparable friends. Miguel had practically tailored his life to fit his son's needs. He'd done everything for him.

Suddenly, out of nowhere, a drunk driver ended Tony's life. And deep inside Miguel felt guilty—he'd been the one driving the jet-boat. The thought that he hadn't taken the proper evasive action tortured him day and night. His inner self concluded that he'd failed to protect his son. And I knew that he felt that way, no matter what he said to other visitors and friends.

Armando Regalado, my wife's older brother, known as Pepe to his friend and family, looked steadily at Raul Padilla. "I found the contact that we were looking for, a Mexican politician who is a personal friend of President Carvajal."

"Who is this Mexican politician?"

"Licensiado Manuel Romero, a very influential politician from Guadalajara, which is the President's power base. Besides, he's member of the Chamber of Deputies."

"Excellent...Can he arrange a meeting with the President?"

"Yes, he said that this weekend would be an ideal time, because the President would be vacationing in Cancun."

"Is that good?"

"He thinks so. He told me that the President would be less busy, more relaxed, and willing to listen to new ideas."

"Today is Wednesday....Okay, tell your friend that we'll be in Cancun this coming Friday. Is that okay with you?"

"Yeah, but before I inform Romero about our arrival date, I

need to notify our friend Emilio of our plan. He wants to participate in this deal."

"Of course, check with him and let me know if there is any problem."

"I sure will. But first, I need to know who is going to pay for my expenses. As you know I am retired."

"Are you? "

"Well not exactly. I'm disabled."

"What happens to you?"

"Three years ago I was involved in a car accident, and it affected my neck. I could not move for two months, it was terrible."

"I don't see anything wrong with you."

"The court ruled in my favor. As long as I can't work, I'll receive a monthly payment from the insurance company."

"Son of a gun...I'll pay your expenses."

The Yucatan peninsula was the seat of the Maya civilization, which was annihilated by a large asteroid that struck their kingdom 600 years before the "discovery" of the Americas by Columbus. Without warning the Mayan empire was struck by a huge ball of fire. Those who survived the initial shock wave witnessed in despair how their God—The Sun—abandon them, and disappeared from the sky. Indeed, the deep darkness that covered their world killed most of the living creatures and all the forests.

In 2077, more than a millennium later, the entire peninsula of Yucatan had become the playground of the Americas.

Emerald green sea water, underground rivers, and Cenotes, are a paradise for pleasure seeking tourists. The nearby islands surrounded by coral reefs add to the feeling of adventure. It is an unforgettable experience to swim in the crystal clear sea waters and feel the close encounter with a school of multicolored fishes.

Pepe and his two friends checked into the Sheraton hotel, on Friday afternoon, 14 May 2077. The Sheraton is strategically located on the Avenue of the Americas. It is right on the beach and across the avenue from the lake, and only one mile down the road from the Presidential retreat.

Shortly after their arrival, Pepe and his two rich friends found their way to the swim-up bar, where they were indulging in Margaritas, Pinas Coladas, and Coco Locos.

"Pepe, where is Romero?" asked Raul, "Did he check-in already?"

"I don't know. Bartender, I need to make a call."

"Barmaid, charge this call to the room of Dr. Armando Regalado," commanded the bartender to the hotel's phone computer.

"I like to talk with Licensiado Manuel Romero. He's suppose to be in Cancun, right here in this hotel."

"Licensiado Romero is not in this hotel," informed the computer.

"Go ahead and check all the five-stars resorts in the Cancun area." Commanded Pepe.

"I cannot find him in any resort. I checked all of them."

"Computer, check the arrivals at the airport for the last three days."

"No , there is no record of his arrival in Cancun."

"Computer call his office in Mexico city, he is a deputy from Guadalajara."

"This is the office of Licensiado Manuel Romero," answered in Spanish Romero's secretary.

"[This is Dr. Regalado, I'm trying to reach Licensiado Romero.]"

"[Licensiado Romero is in Cancun.]"

"[No, he's not. We are down here in Cancun, waiting for him. But he has not checked-in yet at any Hotel in the Cancun area.]"

"[Really! Sorry, but I don't know where else could he be.]"

"[Thank you. Bye.]"

"Computer alert the front desk to call me as soon as Romero arrives."

"I was unaware that you were a doctor," said Emilio. "What kind of doctor are you?"

"I'm an oncologist, I'm board certified in Texas and California." retorted Pepe.

"This is a big fiasco! Do you think Romero is dead?" asked Raul.

"They wouldn't dare to do that," remarked Emilio. "But I suspect that someone just made a large contribution to Romero's electoral fund."

"You are right Emilio, and I don't doubt he is hiding somewhere right here in Cancun," commented Pepe. "I'm sure he's traveling under a different name."

"There must be someone in this town that knows the President well enough to arrange a meeting with him," declared Raul. "Let's go downtown and try to find that guy."

"That is okay with me, but first I need to take a quick shower and change, I'll see you all in the front entrance in a half our," said Emilio.

"It is now one-thirty.... So, let's say that we meet at two o'clock at the front entrance," confirmed Raul.

The three Texans had been to Cancun many times before, and they knew that cab drivers in Cancun double as tourist guides. They are a reliable source of information if you're willing to pay for it.

"[Senor, we want to see the President,]" shouted Raul from the back seat of the taxi.

"[The only thing I can do is drop you off in front of his mansion,]" said the taxi driver.

"[Do you know someone that can arrange a meeting with him,]" insisted Raul.

"[Yes amigo, but it'll cost you fifty dollars plus the fare.]"

"[No problem, senor. We got money.]"

"[In the second floor of the Plaza Caracol there is a jeweler and gem collector that knows the President very well, his name is Jacinto. I believe the name of his shop is El Cenote Verde.]"

"Now you are talking, my friend. Take us there," ordered Raul.

At the end of the 20th century Plaza Caracol had been the center of the action in Cancun, but now, seventy seven years later, it has become an old, dilapidated shopping area where street vendors, young artists, and prostitutes peddle their products. Some Mexicans claim that those vendors can smell the money inside your wallet, and that anything that you tell to anybody will be known by everybody else in matter of seconds.

The Texans were scouting the second floor of Plaza Caracol, when a Mexican shouted at them: "[Senores, what are you looking for?]"

"[A jewelry shop called Cenote Verde,]" answered Pepe.

"[The Cenote Verde went out of business last month,]" responded the man.

"No....That son a of bitch stole our money," complained Raul.

"[Who?]"

"[Never mind.... Do you know Jacinto?]" asked Raul.

"[Yes, I do. What do you want him for?]"

Raul looked to the man with disdain, and was ready to dismiss him, when Emilio intervened, "[We are trying to set up a meeting with the President.]"

"[Jacinto can do it.]"

"[Damned, where the hell is Jacinto?]" retorted Raul.

"[Senor, don't get mad with me, I'm just trying to help.]"

"[Sorry]"

"[He's in Chichen Itza, about a hundred and twenty miles to the west.]"

"[Yes, I know, I had been there,]" said Raul.

The three friends huddled together trying to reach a decision.

"What do you guys think?" asked Raul.

"Let's go, man, before it gets too late. That place is spooky at night time," declared Emilio.

"I agree with him, I don't want to be there after dusk," concurred Pepe.

"[Senor! We want to go there, would you come along?]" asked Raul. "[We will pay you a hundred dollars.]"

"[Sure, I'll go with you. And I know where you can rent an LF jet.]"

"[What is your name?]" Emilio asked.

"Ramon Linares."

"Just a second, I need to eat before we leave this place. Someone is frying empanadas," said Emilio while sniffing the air. "It reminds me of my childhood. I still remember that my grandfather use to take me to eat empanadas at the old Mexican market, on East San Antonio."

On their way out, the group walked through a narrow corridor, bordered by tiny shops with all sort of merchandise. Near the street, under the shade of an old 'ceiba' tree, Emilio found the stand where a young Mexican was cooking and selling 'empanadas.' For a brief moment the three Chicanos forgot about everything else while indulging in empanadas and Dos Equis (XX) beer.

"Wasn't your grandfather one of the founders of New Era?" Raul asked Emilio.

"Yes, he was the first Chairman of the National Executive Committee."

"Then, how come that you are so involved in the annexation movement," said Pepe. "I bet your grandfather would not approve what you are doing."

"Things have changed a lot, these are different times and circumstances, I think he would have approved what I'm doing."

The rental place for LF jets was in a land fill in the middle of the lake, about a half mile southeast from Plaza Caracol. But It was too hot for walking, so they took a taxi.

"Who wants to fly the LF jet?" asked Emilio.

"I know the way there," said Pepe.

"Okay, you are the pilot," said Emilio.

"[Sign here, senor,]" said the attendant pointing to the bottom line in the rental contract. "[Check out time is 3:10 PM]"

"Computer, we want to go to Chichen Itza," commanded Pepe.

"At what time do you want to arrive there?"

"3:30 PM."

"Not possible, maximum cruising speed of this machine is 200 miles per hour."

"Okay...as soon as possible."

"That would be 36 minutes of flying time. We should be there at 3:51."

Without hesitation, Pepe turned on the ignition key, a second later, the LF jet levitated to 20 feet above ground and took off behind a powerful burst of energy. LF jets are short range transporters, relatively slow, but very reliable and easy to handle.

The Texans were fascinated by the thick vegetation of the tropical jungle. "Hard to believe that the Mayans could built so advanced a civilization in this forbidden land," commented Emilio. "And it sure stretches my imagination to think that they were already here in the year 5000 before Christ."

"That jungle is infested with crocodiles and snakes," added Pepe. "Actually the locals believe there are jaguars down there."

"Ramon, where is the landing site?" asked Raul

"[To the east of 'El Castillo,' we are not too far away from it.]" replied Ramon.

The landing site was outside the park, so after landing they took the tourist's shuttle to Chichen Itza.

"Okay Ramon, take us to where Jacinto is," said Raul

"[We need to cut across that wide esplanade in front of 'El Castillo,' and take the trail to the 'Cenote Sagrado',]" explained Ramon.

The trail was very wide but short, less than a thousand feet long. The group, however, walked slowly because the ancient trail was covered with loose rocks and the humidity was unbearable. The air, water vapor would had been a better name, was totally saturated with water in suspension, a hundred percent humidity at 98 degrees.

"[Ramon, what Chichen Itza means,]" asked Pepe.

"[It means, *on the mouth of the well of the witch of the water.]*"

"[Is Jacinto a witch?]"

"[I don't know. You better ask him, we are almost there.]"

The Sacred Cenote, as the locals call it, wasn't a pond, but it wasn't a well either. It was a circular pool, of about two hundred feet in diameter, where the level of the water, which was as green as the surrounding vegetation, was seventy-five feet below the rim of the pool. Ramon explained that the water was roughly seventy feet deep and there was a thick coat of mud in the bottom.

The Sacred Cenote was right there, in front of them. They felt kind of depressed, and all were silent. Finally, Ramon said, "Wait for me here, I'm going to look for Jacinto."

Ramon walked a few feet and went inside a small shed situated right on the edge of the rim. A faint stream of smoke was coming out from a hole in the roof of the tiny structure which was made out of rocks.

After a few minutes, Ramon came out, and said, "Jacinto will see you now."

Jacinto was an old man, his appearance was spiritual, and his demeanor was one of humility. "Welcome to my land," he said in perfect English. "We have been waiting for you, my friends."

"We are glad to be here," responded Raul without really knowing what he was getting into.

Inside the shed, in the middle of the small and only room, there was a big pile of hot rocks. White-hot chunks of coal were placed inside a hollow space formed by the hot rocks. A seeping water bucket hung on top of the pile. Jacinto and Ramon sat on large stones placed close to one side of the pile of rocks; the Chicanos sat on smaller stones at the other side of the pile.

"How come you were waiting for us?" asked Raul.

Jacinto's spiritual calmness evoked mystical feelings in the Chicanos as his gaze floated in the vapor-filled room. After a while he said, "My friends, you are in a very special place for a very important reason. This is the only magnetic eye left on Earth, and we brought you here because we need your help."

"Just a second, we came here looking for your help," contended Raul. "Ramon told us that you can arrange for us a meeting with the President."

"Sorry, it's my fault," said Jacinto. "I'll arrange the meeting for you."

"Wait, I'd like to know what is so special about this place," protested Pepe, "and what is a magnetic eye?"

"Raul, you're an asshole," swore Emilio. "You cut Jacinto off when he was in the middle of an extraordinary revelation. Stupid!"

"It's not his fault," declared Jacinto. "Yum Kimil, the master of the world of the dead was speaking for him. You better leave now, before is too late."

"What about the meeting with the President?" asked Pepe.

"Be at the main gate of the presidential retreat tomorrow morning at 10:15. Tell the guards that Jacinto send you, and that you want to speak with the President," replied Jacinto.

"Ramon, are you coming with us?" asked Raul.

"No, go ahead without me," replied Ramon. "I'm safe. Don't worry, everything is under control. I will be there when you need me."

"Where?"

"Anywhere."

"Here, take the one hundred dollars that I owe you," said Raul while handing the money to Ramon.

"A real paper bill! Hard to see real money now a days. Thank you," responded Ramon, as his wide face lighted up with an ear to ear smile.

The presidential security officers were unfriendly, and unimpressed when Pepe mentioned the name of Jacinto, yet they gained access to the 'Federales' bungalow. There, an inquisitive security man questioned them. The Chicanos spent the next half hour listening to a summary of their lives, as recounted by the Federales' computer, that was connected to the Master Spy Computer of the Mexican intelligence services. After long silent stares, and after consulting with some civilian higher-ups, they were cleared to see the President. They were escorted to the main structure of the presidential retreat complex by a tall, mustached security officer, and three weapon carrying presidential guards.

They walked in silence, under the merciless tropical sun, toward the front entrance of the splendid mansion. The eleven thousand square feet structure blended surprisingly well with the surrounding terrain. In true Mayan tradition, it was made out of large cut stones, cream colored, and so well fitted and set that it was hard to see the joints. The men crossed a very colorful garden full of tropical plants and landscaping ponds filled with rare colored fishes.

In front of the mansion they came to a flight of steps which they quickly climbed with simulated determination. Flanking the double leaf imposing door were two presidential guards who snapped a military salute. Once inside the front foyer they encountered a civilian, who was wearing a shining white linen suit. The man spoke briefly with the security officer and then introduced himself as a presidential aide.

"Why do you want to see the President?"

"We have a very important proposition for him," responded

Raul.

"What kind of proposition?"

"Sorry, but our proposition is only for your President. We will not discuss it with anyone else," said Emilio, "You can tell the President that it's in relation to Texas. And you can mention my name....I'm sure he heard about me."

"Your name is Emilio Cardona, isn't?"

"Yes."

The three Texan-Chicanos waited a couple of minutes before the presidential aide came back and led them into a big room in the second level of the mansion. The furniture was informal, but the ambiance prevailing on the room was of unadulterated luxury. Through the window panels in the northwest wall, they could see a large terrace, and farther beyond the emerald green ocean waters, a white sandy beach. A large three-decked yacht was moored at the mansion pier.

With no hint of pretentious pomp President Carvajal came into the room. He was an slender man, in his late forties. His large nose resting on a large black mustache dominated his facial expression. He looked friendly and jovial. After shaking hands with the visitors, the informally attired president asked, "[What I can do for you in the next ten minutes?]"

"[Mister President, It would take more than ten minutes to explain everything to you,]" declared Emilio.

"[You better start your presentation, I am going scuba diving in ten minutes, no matter what.]"

"We believe that the majority of the people in Texas, our native state, have reached the conclusion that they would be better off as part of Mexico than as part of the United States. So if Mexico wants Texas, we will start a campaign to convince the other states within the union that it's in their best interest to let Texas go."

The President looked at his visitors in disbelief, then he finally said, "You're right, it will take more than ten minutes." The President activated the room's computer and advised his yacht captain that he would be late for the scuba diving trip.

"Is New Era behind this?" asked the President.

"No, New Era wants to stay in the Union," replied Pepe.

"So, what political party is advocating Texas annexation to Mexico?"

Emilio hesitated for a second, took a deep breath, then looked for a go ahead signal from his friends, and said:

"Mister President, the political situation in Texas isn't that simple, it never has been. The Governor actively supports a movement that is working toward Texas' independence. Obviously he wants to become the first president of the new nation. He sees himself like a new Sam Houston or George Washington. The independence movement is very popular in Texas, and right now is leading in all the opinion polls against the two other alternatives—staying in the Union or annexation to Mexico. But we believe that we can turn the public opinion around. We can set up an office to accomplish that goal. We have the money, the organization, and the management skills to do it. The only thing we don't have is your consent. We want to know if you are willing to advocate this solution, and what are Mexico's terms for the annexation. There is one thing that is not open to negotiation. In true Texan tradition we reserve the right to quit our union with Mexico at any time that the

Texas nation so desire."

The Mexican president, paced the room, in silence, forward and backward several times. He gazed at the ocean for a couple of minutes without really focusing in anything. Finally, he turned around, returned to the middle of the room, and facing his visitors said:

"Mexico has been looking forward to this proposal since 1836, when Texas declared independence from us. So, this subject reaches very deeply into the conscience of the Mexican nation. We felt betrayed and humiliated. But worst of all, was the overwhelming sense of impotence. The unbearable fact that we lost an immense territory, half of our nation, without really defending it.

"All along regaining Texas has been our goal, our dream. But, I don't believe you are ready for it, yet. True, Latins are the largest ethnic group in Texas, but not by much. The Anglos are close behind. So, I am not too sure that Texas will directly go from been a State of the Union to be a Province of Mexico.

"We know that Texas wants to become independent. So the two step annexation to Mexico is far more practical and safer. Yes, my friends, Texas will become first independent, and then it will join Mexico, where it belongs.

"Relations between Mexico and the U.S.A. are better now than ever before, and since the year 2010 Mexico has enjoyed an spectacular economical growth. We are now a fully developed, and very rich country. We don't want to risk all the things that we had accomplished in the 21st century by going to war with the USA.

"My dear friends, you are rich and powerful men, well

connected entrepreneurs. But it took a long time, and the sweat and perseverance of countless Mexican peasants to produce what you are. You, and millions like you, are the product of a historical event of giant proportions. For more than two centuries the Mexican people have endured discrimination in our own land, we have been ignored as if we never existed, we had worked hard and long for meager salaries. Now, at the end of the journey, we cannot afford to be in a hurry. We are going to do the right thing at the right time. Besides, this is Mexico's time, and I'm enjoying every minute of it. No, I'm not interested in your proposal, not yet, but I love you for proposing it."

The President's statement inspired the three Chicanos. Suddenly they acquired a historical perspective, which revealed to them the fine details of the present. They could now justify their urge, explain their motive, and see the truth behind the wrinkles of time.

"Mr. President, we understand your position and accept your decision," said Emilio. "Although you rejected our proposal, there is happiness in our hearts, and we leave wiser than when we arrived. We thank you for it."

The President stepped forward and shook hands with the visitors, and just before departing casually asked, "What is your connection with Jacinto?"

"A taxi driver told us that he could arrange a meeting with you. But, Ramon Linares was the one that took us to see him," replied Pepe.

"How was your meeting with Jacinto?"

"Strange...weird," said Pepe. "He said that the Sacred Cenote was the only magnetic eye left on Earth. We had been wondering about that."

"The name magnetic eye is misleading. The small, localized disturbance of the Earth magnetic field in that location is only a secondary effect of a much larger and unique phenomenon prevailing inside the Sacred Cenote," explained the President.

"Really...what is it?" asked Emilio.

"Oh, no, my friend. I wouldn't dare to reveal the mystery to you. Only an Itzae can do that," said the President on his way out.

7 What do I do?

The funeral services for Tony were held at St Francis Church on Saturday, 15 May 2077. He was buried at the Southwest Memorial cemetery. After the grave side service, my wife and I attended a get-together for family and friends at the St. Francis School cafeteria. The cafeteria's room was ill-suited for this kind of gathering, it was too large and full of tables and chairs. But the guests, mostly Tony's school mates and their parents, felt at home. The food matched very well the attendance—trays of cup-cakes, chips, and hastily put together sandwiches were resting on four tables which had been paper dressed and lined up end-to-end at one side of the room. The centerpiece of the food display was a huge bowl of an orange looking refreshment. We found some loose chairs at the opposite end of the room and sat there close to a wooden stage; apparently the cafeteria was also the school theater.

Before leaving we approached Xiomara to express our sympathy and support. She stood a few feet away from us, talking with a couple of ladies. We waited until the ladies seemed to be finished, although they remained close by. My wife offered her condolences first, speaking of divine intervention in our daily life, and expressed the grief she felt for the bereaved mother.

I tried to convey my concern for her, and said, “You can visit us any time you want. Don’t worry about bothering us, we’re not that busy.”

“I don’t feel much like visiting,” Xiomara said, grief overflowing her words. Before she could say anything else, one of the ladies, interrupted the conversation, and said to me, “I would be delighted to visit you any time, at any place.”

The young lady looked directly into my eyes. She was smiling and her eyes sparkled with an alluring and challenging message. She was flirting with me, right in front of my wife and the deceased mother! I felt embarrassed, but I enjoyed the moment and appreciated the young lady’s unrestrained candor. We never were introduced, so I didn’t learn her name or anything else about her, except that she was too young for me. We left immediately after that, without noticing that I had left my hat on the rear of the room.

During the trip back home, I couldn’t talk to Marta without thinking about the young lady I just met. I felt bewitched by her remark and charmed by the sparks in her eyes. I wondered if I’d ever see her again.

I was resigned to endure the heavy burden of a bad marriage, because I was committed with great passion to the cause of keeping Texas within the union, and that took most of my energy and time. Things, however, were much better when I was younger and building up a family. But now that the children had grown and left home, I felt a deep void in my relationship with Marta. First, I thought that the problem with our marriage was lack of communication, that somehow we could fix it, if we really talked to each other. Yet, after painful introspection during the last two years, I came to realize that Marta had never really bonded with me, that we were two separate persons living together by the interest created during twenty four years of marriage. It was a sad conclusion, yet it never prevented me from being an excellent husband. Because Marta at forty five was still a beautiful woman. She was tall and slender, and had a perfect set of teeth. Her hair, however, wasn't as silky and shiny as it used to be. Her demeanor didn't match her figure. She didn't have any flair and hated classy or expensive places. She looked like a cover girl but acted like a mail woman of a rural district. All our friends thought that we were the perfect couple. This was reinforced by Marta's ability for projecting wholesome images. This was specially true with new acquaintances. She was very nice with everybody else, except me.

On Sunday, early in the afternoon, I returned to St. Francis to pick up my hat. A big meeting was going on in the cafeteria. A priest was addressing a group of about fifty people. My hat was directly behind the podium, on the wooden stage, close to the wall. Instead of turning right and going directly to where my hat was, I turned left, toward a set of swing doors. I pushed them open and found myself on the middle of the kitchen. There, to my surprise and wonder, I was greeted by the same ladies that I encountered the day before. I made eye contact with the young lady, the same one that wanted to visit me any time, at any place, and asked, “Are you a cook or a teacher?”

“I don’t know what I am.” Her voice was low and she sounded dejected.

“You must be something.”

“I’m a helper.”

And she looked like one. She was poorly dressed with baggy clothes of no particular color. The other lady was chubby, and more in control of herself.

I introduced myself. “I am Ernesto Tellez, but my friends call me Tito.”

“Glad to meet you formally,” she said while shaking my hand. “My name is Jenny...Jenny Douglas.”

“I’m Sharon Woods,” said the chubby lady. “We’re preparing food for the underprivileged. And you, Mr. Tellez, what do you do?”

“I work for New Era, the political party. I’m the chairman of the National Executive Committee.

Meanwhile, Jenny walked away in the direction of a side door. That part of the kitchen was poorly lit, but I still could see her, with the corner of my eye, reclined against the bottom portion of the door, which had been sliced in the middle for the benefit of the kitchen traffic. I joined her and asked, "Are you okay?"

She turned around, looked at me enticingly, and whined in almost a whisper. "I don't know what I am going to do."

I didn't answered immediately, because I didn't know what she was talking about. But I sensed that she was in distress. Instead, I just said, while pointing toward the wooden stage, "Can you see my hat over there?"

Trying to spot the hat, she tilted her head closer to mine. We were side by side, real cozy in the dim light .

"No," she finally responded.

"Look...behind the podium...." I pointed again.

"Yeah, I can see it now."

"What do you think...should I go and get it?"

"Go for it." Her dark green eyes, had become irresistibly alluring and seductive.

I wasn't sure of what she meant, but I sure made the right move. We embraced and kissed, as if it were the final and only kiss of our life. It was an erotic and desperate kiss, it was an eruption of primitive desires hidden in the deepest portion of our brains for too long, and suddenly liberated by the realization that, finally, we had found the right match.

"Are you for real?" I asked in disbelief.

"Yes...listen to my heart...convinced?"

I didn't answer, instead I looked long into her eyes. Something about this lady was very appealing to me, but I didn't know what. However, the intensity of my feelings toward her made me feel delightfully warm and carefree, and that was enough for me. I was absolutely convinced, and lucky to be so.

"Jenny, I need you here," shouted Sharon.

I walked close to the wall in order not to disturb the priest's lecture, got my hat and returned to where Jenny was. She was gone, nowhere in sight.

Pondering the situation, on my way back home, I was fascinated by the precise and easy conversation with the lady helper...who unexpectedly became the object of my desire. I speculated that she was a poor lady trying to make ends meet, possibly a divorcee. Then I realized that I failed to set up a date with Jenny, and that I knew almost nothing about her, couldn't even remember her last name.

The encounter with Jenny suddenly changed my outlook for the remainder of my life. Again, my heart was full of anticipation, enthusiasm. I was alive, really alive. But, now that I was reaching home, the feelings of euphoria and passion changed to concern and guilt. I became disgusted with myself. I thought that I was a gutless creature who was afraid of his wife. I worried about what she might do if she found out about my encounter with Jenny. In the middle of a tantrum, she always insulted me without mercy, and made wild assertions to hurt me as much as she could. I hated the idea of facing Marta in those conditions. But it happened so many times before that her insults didn't effect me anymore, which only made her angrier.

The fact that for many years I put up with this despicable verbal abuse made me feel very bad about myself. I did it to maintain our family union, for the sake of my future grandchildren. I wanted to grow old surrounded by them.

The prospect of lying to Marta worried me, but I concluded that it was absolutely necessary. Because if she found out that I was fooling around with Jenny, she would become hysterical and shortly after that she would become verbally abusive and violent. It wasn't realistic to assume that I could fool her, because she trusted no one, and was always alert. Besides, she witnessed Jenny's flirtation with me, so she would be looking for any hint that I am being unfaithful to her.

I knew that I was the guilty party, and I was ashamed of it. Yet, when I reached home I acted as normal as I could, as if nothing had happened, and I was extra nice to Marta. Deep inside, however, I felt remorse and wished nothing had really happened.

"Honey...I brought fresh vegetables from the Farmer's Market, as you asked me to," I shouted from the kitchen, while placing the vegetables on the counter.

"Did you find your hat?" she shouted from the bedroom in the upper level.

"Yes, it was in the same place that I left it yesterday."

"Master Tito, I have a message for you. I could not reach you at the car because you left the link open," reported my HK (Home Keeper) computer over the kitchen's speakers.

"Home Keeper, deliver the message in my office," I commanded, while walking toward my office.

"Ruben Vargas called. He wants you to call him back, right away."

"Okay, put him on."

HK displayed my friend's image on the high definition computer/TV screen mounted on the wall of my private office.

"Ruben, what is up?"

"We need to have a private conversation," replied Ruben. "Let's get together for lunch."

"It is kind of late...almost two o'clock," I contended. "Where do you want to go for lunch?"

"The same place we went last month, do you remember?"

"Okay, I'll see you there in thirty minutes," I replied.

"Home keeper, did somebody else have access to Ruben's message?" I inquired after talking with Ruben.

"I don't know, master."

"Did somebody else scan your short term memory after you received Ruben's call?"

"Yes, someone did...it happened one minute after Ruben called."

"Computer HK29, retrace that scan."

"Master Tito, the scan request came through my telephonic port and it was originated in downtown San Antonio."

"HK29, erase from all your memories Ruben's last call and this conversation with me."

"Done."

"Thank you."

"You're welcome."

"Marta...I am leaving, I need to see Ruben right away," I yelled in my way out.

It was fifteen past two when I arrived to the restaurant. I asked the hostess for Ruben and she directed me toward a booth in the bar area.

"Howdy."

"Please, sit down my friend," said Ruben. "Listen, I'm sorry that I made you to come all the way down here in such a short notice."

"You got that right. What's so important that it couldn't wait?"

The waitress came before Ruben could answer. She said a few friendly words and then asked for our order.

"I'm going to have 'Today's Special,' yellow rice mixed with finely chopped parsley, minced garlic, and chopped fried egg-whites. And a soup of black-beans," ordered Ruben.

"Your open face enchilada, what is in it?" I asked.

"It's chunks of turkey pastrami, pieces of red bell pepper, and finely chopped cilantro on a rye tortilla," answered the waitress.

"Yes, I want that. Bring me also gaspacho de broccoli, and coffee."

"Your brother-in-law is the problem," declared Ruben point blank. "He and two influential business men went to see the Mexican president."

"What about?"

"I don't know for sure, but apparently they went there to propose the annexation of Texas to Mexico," replied Ruben.

"No!...They can't do that. Who the hell they think they are?"

"Don't be so sure, I think they can do it, provided they have enough votes to amend the Texas constitution," argued Ruben.

"That's precisely the problem, less than ten percent of the voters would support that amendment. Besides, the United

States wouldn't allow that."

"I think it is legally possible," contended Ruben. "I need to confirm this, but I believe that Texas is the only state that can leave the union, if Texans so desire."

"Who are the other two men who went with him?"

"Raul Padilla, the owner of the largest cement plant in Texas, and Emilio Cardona. He owns a plant that manufactures silicon wafers, one of the largest in the world."

"I can imagine the motive of those two renegades, but I don't know why my brother-in-law is supporting that vile idea."

"He's a big jerk, that is why. We need to attack that proposal, before it's too late. Many of our citizens are first generation Mexican-American, and I'm sure a great number of them would be happy to see Texas incorporated into Mexico," declared Ruben.

"Also, some Anglos, mostly of them descendent from the original settlers, are in favor of incorporating Texas to the Mexican Republic," I argued.

"I know, there was no unanimity in the 1845's annexation to the U.S.A.," affirmed Ruben. "Tito, you must explain to the New Era politicians what is going on here. We must start a campaign to discredit that idea as soon as possible."

"Agree, I'll do that first thing Monday..."

I paused when I realized that Ruben was not listening. "What's wrong?" I asked.

"Tito, don't look now, but there are a couple of guys sitting on the first table on my right, they look very suspicious to me. I caught one of them staring at us," said Ruben. "They look weird, like members of a satanic cult."

"Come on, Ruben...don't turn paranoid on me. They sure look weird. But members of a satanic cult? I always knew you've a vivid imagination, but this is ridiculous."

"You may be right, but I'd feel much better if we paid and leave," insisted Ruben.

"Okay."

"Where did you go?" asked my wife.

"I went to see Ruben. He left an urgent message with HK. He wanted to see me right away."

"Did you have lunch with him?"

"Yes."

"So, I stay here, working all day long, while you were having a good time with your friend."

"I'm sorry, but it was a very important problem that required my immediate attention."

"Do you think I'm your maid? Cynic...You are like your mother, taking advantage of everybody else!" shouted Marta while pushing me out of her way and picking up her car key.

"Where are you going?"

"Why don't you ask your friend, the wino...drunkard!"

8 The Sacred Cenote

On Wednesday, June 2, 2077, Marta and I attended a concert of the New York Philharmonic Orchestra at the San Antonio de Valero Theater in the new convention center at HemisFair Plaza.

I was flabbergasted when I saw Jenny sitting two rows ahead of me. She looked radiant, which contrasted with her escort whom I guessed was her husband. He looked somber and withdrawn. His teeth were disgustedly stained and his expensive formal attire couldn't cover the fact that his body needed an urgent overhaul—narrow shoulders, wide hips.

That day I realized that I'd misjudged her circumstances. Jenny wasn't a poor young lady trying to make ends meet. On the contrary, she seemed to be well-to-do and very self-assured. She was exquisitely dressed and well coiffured, which gave her a sophisticated appearance. A couple of times I caught her turning her head, looking back out of the corner of her eyes toward where I sat.

My wife was with me, so I didn't have the opportunity to greet her, nor could I inquire from anyone about her family name. During the intermission I saw her in the lobby, talking with her friend Sharon.

When Marta and I got home, we found Pepe waiting for us.

"Who let you in?" I asked.

"Nobody, Marta gave me the door's PIN number," Pepe said.

I looked to my wife. "How could you do that without telling me?

"This is my house, too. I don't need your permission to do anything. He's my brother!"

Marta had always been very protective of her family. She always protected them from me, as if somehow I were going to hurt them. But when Pepe divorced some years ago and moved closer to us the problem got much worse. He visited our home frequently, almost every week, and oftentimes Marta asked him to stay overnight. She became very dependent of his counseling. I was losing authority in my own house. I enjoyed Pepe's company and conversation because he was a very smart man who engaged in strange activities and ideas. He was promiscuous without shame and antisocial without remorse. It didn't affect me, but he was destroying his sister.

"Tito, I brought empanadas and wine," Pepe said. "Go ahead and try them. They're delicious."

"Marta, you make decisions that affect my life without telling me," I said.

Incapable of a rational dialogue, Marta replied in her usual offensive manner. I could never get a point across to her. She always turned the conversation into an insult contest. "Don't close your eyes when you are talking, you look like your sister Ortensia. You look like her, because she's your mother. Go ahead and call your niece, she's so nice. . . ."

After the verbal barrage, Marta locked herself in our bedroom.

I took a couple bites of empanada, and sat besides Pepe who was watching the news on the recreation room's TV.

"This empanada is delicious. Where did you buy it?"

"At the Bayside Marina, where I keep my boat in Corpus Christi."

"Did you find the guy who sabotaged your boat?"

"No, but I know who did it." Pepe turned to face me.

"Who?"

"A redneck who works in a fire station near the Marina."

"Did you tell the police?" I took a swallow of wine, but kept my attention on his face.

"Yes...yesterday, when I called the police because somebody scratched my car's paint."

"Really? How bad was it?"

"I counted thirteen scratches on the driver's side door and on the roof."

This was not the first time that I heard Pepe portraying himself as being persecuted by sinister characters. He often saw himself as the victim of powerful forces that for not clear reasons were attacking him. So I was not alarmed by his story, and like many times before I went along with him. I always considered Pepe an expert in creating complicated plots.

"What did the police say about the redneck?"

"They need some proof before they can arrest him."

"Why is he doing this to you?"

"He's a Satan's Witness. I believe the cult wants to punish me."

"Why?"

"I joined them and they were delighted with my knowledge and interpretation of the Bible."

"You conned the Satan's Witness? Man, you have guts!"

"That's not all. They introduced me to Cindy, and I married her within two weeks. She was so beautiful."

"Cindy **was?** What happened to her?"

"She disappeared. She's been gone for more than two months."

"Did you report that to the police?"

"Yes. The police couldn't find her. And the Satan's Witness believe that I killed her, and that is why they are chasing me."

I had to ask. "Did you?"

"No! I loved her! Couldn't have loved her more, but it wasn't enough for her. She was only twenty-six years old, no way I could satisfy her. Actually, we only lived together for ten days. You know what? She told me that she was very interested in meeting you. In fact, she disappeared the day before we were supposed to come to San Antonio and meet you. Would you believe, she left me for a Gypsy?"

"No, I don't believe any of that. Let me have more of that wine," I took a sip and changed the subject. "How was your trip to Cancun?"

"Fine," Pepe poured some wine for himself. "President Carvajal is a likable man, very smart and sincere. The real surprise was Jacinto."

"Who is Jacinto?"

"He is an Itzae, a witch that we met at the Sacred Cenote in Chichen Itza."

"Why did he surprise you?"

"It was more what he told us that surprised me. Jacinto said they need our help, that was the reason why they brought us to the Cenote. He added that the Sacred Cenote is the only magnetic eye left on the planet Earth. He was about to reveal a very important secret when Raul interrupted him."

"So what? What's the big deal?"

"We aren't sure, but according to President Carvajal, who knows Jacinto very well, the disturbance of the Earth's magnetic field around the Sacred Cenote is only a secondary effect of a unique physical phenomenon taking place inside the cenote."

"What does Jacinto look like?"

"He's a mystic. Very spiritual. A very intriguing being."

"Being? What do you mean by that?"

"I don't know, but he has a non-human quality. He's weird. He looks like some kind of creature."

"Amazing. But after listening to your revelations I feel an irresistible urge to go there and talk directly with Jacinto. I must find more about the unique physical phenomenon President Carvajal alluded to. Where I can reach Raul?"

"He lives right here in San Antonio. His company phone number is 111-3555."

The next day, Thursday, June 3, I called Raul from my New York office. "Mr. Padilla, this is Ernesto Tellez..." He interrupted me before I could finish the sentence.

"I know exactly who you are," he said. "The chairman of New Era's National Executive Committee. What can I do for you?"

"This call has nothing to do with politics," I said. "I'm a nuclear physicist and I'm very interested in the Sacred Cenote and what Jacinto and President Carvajal said about it."

"Your brother-in-law keeps you well informed."

"Mr. Padilla, my interest in the Sacred Cenote is only scientific. I must find out what kind of unique physical phenomenon is taking place inside the Sacred Cenote. I'd been trying to prove the existence of time-warped space-time for many years and the Sacred Cenote might provide the evidence I'm looking for. I became interested in the structure of space-time while doing research work at the Austin particle accelerator. But if you don't want to talk I'll understand."

After that exchange, he changed his attitude toward me and he verified Pepe's account of their trip to Cancun.

I was about to leave for lunch, when the computer alerted me that I had an incoming call.

"Who's calling?"

"*A friend,*" replied the computer.

"What kind of friend?"

"*A lonesome helper.*"

"Put her on the screen," I told the computer.

"Jenny! I'm so glad you called."

"Really? I was wondering what happened to you." Her voice wasn't firm and her dark-green eyes were irresistibly alluring and seductive.

"Where are you?"

"Right here in the lobby of your building."

"My darling, I'm coming right down. It'll take only a couple of minutes. I can't wait to see you."

The second the door opened, I bulldozed my way out of the elevator. She rushed into my arms, and we embraced and kissed as the lunch crowd passed by. She looked down and noticed that I was aroused. I blushed and felt embarrassed. "Excuse me," I said. "This never happened to me so suddenly."

"Don't be ashamed. It's my fault," she said. "Besides, I like it."

We left the building laughing with our arms around each other waists.

"Where shall we go?" I asked.

"Any place you want."

"Let's go to the Golden Empire Hotel. Is that okay with you?"

"Yes, but isn't it too fancy?"

"Yes, but it's the only one nearby. I don't want to take a taxi. Cab's drivers are notorious paid informers of the media."

As soon as the room's door closed we became possessed by an erotic demon. We locked lips while moving rhythmically. Her pussy was hot and her tits hard. She wasn't looking in my eyes, she wanted to fuck immediately. We ripped off each other clothes, and without taking off the elaborate cover she jumped on the huge bed. She opened her legs and while squeezing and caressing her breasts shouted, "help me!" Her clitoris was pink and gooey, it was palpitating, it could not wait any longer. I nailed her hard and repeatedly, each time faster. We came along at the same time. Her orgasm was noisy and full of guilt, it sounded like a lament more than the culmination of a wild sex experience.

In the back of my mind, I worried because I was supposed to be back in the office at one-thirty. When Jenny went to the bathroom, I called the office.

"Rafi, I need a favor," I said.

"Are you at the Golden Empire Hotel?"

"How do you know?"

"I saw you and your girl friend in the lobby of our building."

"Please, listen to me. I don't have much time."

"Ah ha! You are in between sessions. I bet she's in the bathroom."

"Cut it out! I can't attend the one-thirty meeting with the advertising agency people. I want you to chair the meeting. Please tell my secretary that I'll be late returning from lunch. Let her know that I'm fine, but nothing else. Understood?"

"Relax, old buddy and enjoy life. No big deal. I'll cover for you."

Jenny joined me in the bedroom and began getting dressed.

I said, "I'm hungry. Let's order some lunch."

"I'm hungry, too. I think an snack would be better, because I need to be back in San Antonio at four o'clock."

"Whatever you want, my darling."

She suggested seafood hors-d'œuvres. I ordered them along with French champagne and espresso.

I opened the door leading to the balcony. The view from the fifty-ninth floor of the Golden Empire Hotel was breathtaking. We were in our private space, but the time seemed unreal, a figment of our imagination, and we knew that it was coming to an end. Jenny didn't want to let it go. She clung to my arm and her illusions. She asked, "Do you like New York?"

"I love it," I said. "Wouldn't it be lovely if we both could move to New York?"

"Is that a proposition?"

"No, just a dream."

The sound of the computer bell, alerting us that someone was at the door, brought us back to reality. The bell boy had brought the food. It was more of a feast than the light lunch we'd asked for.

When I returned to the office, my secretary told me that Luis Santamarina, the junior senator from Texas, wanted to see me. He'd left a message on my computer. Luis was my personal friend and the frontrunner candidate to the U.S. presidency. I called him back immediately.

"Tito, we need to do something about the Texas' Independence Drive," said the Senator. "The movement is becoming stronger every day."

"We are expending more than we can afford in this campaign. We have funds for one more week only," I said.

"Use as much money as you need, my friend. Don't try to save on this one. Both the Democrats and Republicans are willing to contribute money for the campaign to keep Texas in the union."

"That's great, but they also need to increase their effort within Texas itself. Each party must have their most likable spokesmen touring the state every day until the day of the referendum."

"I agree. I'll let them know," declared the Senator. "I want you to get more support from academia and the 'intelligentsia' of the rest of the country."

"We have been initiating, promoting, and paying for their appearance in TV talk shows from the very beginning. And we've been paying for the unconditional support of countless syndicated columnists. We have the written media one hundred percent covered."

"The entire congressional delegation from Texas, thirty six members strong is having a crucial meeting at eleven o'clock tomorrow morning in the south wing of the Capitol. We invited the governor of Texas and he's coming. I need you here."

"I'd like to bring along the director of our historical research group. Is that okay?"

"Good thinking. As you know, the governor has the support of the Daughters of the Republic of Texas, and they are very well informed in the history of early Texas."

Thursday, 3 June 2077, was a very important day in my life. The events forced me to make crucial decisions both in my personal life and in my professional career. However, I realized that my life was insignificant compared to the future of an entire nation. My country demanded the best of me. I was determined to perform my duties as best as I could. Marta and Jenny would have to wait until I had time to break our romantic triangle.

That night, on my way to the New York City apartment

which I shared with Rafi, I examined the political situation. New Era's immediate objective was to win the congressional election of 2078, and then go for the presidency in the general election of 2080. I never solicited the support of the extreme right because I thought their support could destroy New Era's political image. I believed we could defeat the Texas Independence Referendum without the help of the extreme right. I hated to even think we were supporting the same cause. My gut feeling told me their help could produce more harm than good. But the reality was that we could not possible win the presidential election without Texas. In the grand scheme of things, it was crucial to defeat the Texas Independence Referendum. Against my advice, New Era's decision makers decided to embrace the extreme right and go along with them.

The following morning I was walking toward the underpass, below the steps in front of the capitol facade facing east, when I heard someone shouting at me. "Senor, Senor!"

I turned around and saw someone walking fast toward me, I stopped and shouted back to him in Spanish, "What do you want?"

"[Please Mister, wait for me,]" said the stranger.

"[Okay, but hurry up. I don't have time to waste.]"

"[I want to offer you a free trip to Mexico.]"

"[Where in Mexico?]"

"[Cancun. You will stay in the Silver Shell, a five star resort, for a week. All expenses paid.]"

The stranger was now standing on front of me.

"[What are you selling?]"

"[Time-share units.]"

"[I not interested...]" I was interrupted in by the unmistakable sound of a semi-automatic weapon being fired.

Instinctively, we hit the ground. A few seconds later, I heard someone yelling for help. I stood up and saw several Capitol guards running toward the underpass. One of them stopped and asked, "What are you doing here?"

"I'm going to a meeting of the Texas Congressional Caucus. I'm the chairman of New Era's National Executive Committee"

"Are you a member of the Congress?"

"No."

"And who are you?" the guard asked to the stranger.

"I am a salesman, I sell time-share units," the stranger said in Spanish. "I am a Mexican citizen."

The guard acted like he wasn't sure what to do with the stranger. He called for instructions. Immediately after, he handcuffed the stranger. Then he asked me, "Do you know this guy?"

"Not really, Officer. But I can assure you that he was talking to me when all this happened. We heard the sound of gunfire and dropped to the ground."

Another guard showed up. He placed my identification card inside a hand-held ID card reader and asked me to put the thumb of my right hand on top of the finger print verification square. A minute later he let me go. Before leaving, I asked: "What happened?"

"Someone assassinated the governor of Texas."

For a minute I was perplexed, paralyzed, and incapable of reacting. Finally, the sounds of the emergency vehicles converging on the Capitol brought me to life. I climbed the steps in front of the Capitol and tried to enter. Two guards stopped me and adamantly told me to leave immediately.

On my way to the closest Metro station, I called Senator Santamarina. He was upset and told me that the meeting had been canceled. He stated that the impact of the Governor's assassination on Texas politics would be profound and unpredictable.

Before entering the Metro station, I called Marta. She'd already heard the news about the Governor's assassination. Our HK computer, which is always on line, had brought her a special bulletin from one of the news channels. She was alarmed and sad. "What do you think is going to happen now?"

"I don't know."

"When are you coming home?"

"I'm on my way there. I arrived in Washington this morning, so I don't need to check out of any hotel. I'm taking the subway to Metro Center, and then I'll connect with the Orange Line. That will take me directly into the transcontinental shuttle station. Bye-bye, sweetheart."

9 Only Space, No Time

Friday, 4 June 2077

Back home, I explained to Marta what happened to me in front of the Capitol. How strange indeed it was. "I wouldn't be here talking to you, if it not were for the time-share salesman who stopped me at the precise moment, then kept talking to me."

"Do you know his name? Where is he now?" Marta asked.

"He might be in jail, because they took him away handcuffed."

"What are you going to do?"

"I need to find out where he is. If he's in jail, I'll help him as much as I can. It's the least I can do."

"Watch out, he could be involved in the Governor's assassination."

"I don't think so, but I could be wrong. So, I'll investigate this a little further before taking any action."

"Honey, you need to be more careful. I don't want to lose you," said Marta in her best voice.

I was surprised by her loving words and concern. I interpreted them as a sign that she recognized that she'd been unfair with me. I didn't know how long her transformation will last, but I welcomed it anyway. I knew it wasn't a calculated move, she wasn't that kind of woman. She could be aggressive, abusive and irrational. But she wasn't a foxy lady.

I had always admired my wife slender body. Her long, delicate legs were exquisitely shaped. And her tits were still firm, of the right size and with no ugly veins. Her beautiful face was framed by black wavy hair. She was an imposing beauty. But her facial expression was firm and resolute and her eyes weren't tender. So, her words sounded a little out of sync. They were indeed rare. Never before had Marta allowed herself to express any concern about my wellbeing. But I was an easy prey to anything resembling security. Suddenly, I felt the urge of having sex with Marta. It was the natural thing to do, after all she was my wife. It was great, intense and amorous, but it felt funny. Afterward, I thought of myself as a low life who was cheating on his wife. The idea of terminating my marriage to Marta scared me. I realized that I was ambivalent and behaving like a spineless jerk, that the honest thing to do was to break with Jenny.

Full of confidence, after the sex pause, I sprung into action. "HK, I need a summary of the news related to the assassination of the Governor of Texas. It happened today. Specifically, I want to know about any suspect or detainee they have on custody."

"They do not have too many leads. They suspect that the perpetrators could be connected with one of the many militia groups now operating in the country. But nothing firm yet. The police detained a Mexican citizen, called Ramon Linares. He lives in Cancun, Mexico and was here as a tourist. According to the police, he was talking with Ernesto Tellez, that is you, Master, when the shooting occurred. He was released for lack of concrete evidence tying him to the crime."

"When was he released?"

"At 3:44 PM, Eastern Time, almost five hours ago."

"HK, check all the airports in the Washington Metropolitan area. I want to find out if Ramon Linares left the country, and if he did, where he went."

"He took Mexicana flight 226 out of Baltimore-Washington International Airport for Cancun, Mexico at 6:55 PM, Eastern Time."

Next day, early Saturday morning, I was on my way to Cancun, a short hour from San Antonio. The Mexicana airliner cruised at 1300 miles per hour, close to twice the speed of the sound. I looked out of the plane's window but I didn't see any of the scenery below. I was totally intrigued by the life-saving encounter I'd had with Ramon, and by Pepe's revelation regarding the Sacred Cenote. He'd mentioned that according to Jacinto, the Sacred Cenote was the only magnetic eye left on the planet Earth. And I was intrigued by Jacinto's statement that they brought Pepe and his friend to the Sacred Cenote because they needed their help. What unique physical phenomenon was President Carvajal talking about?

The Cancun International Airport always had been a difficult place for me. This time, however, I went through customs in record time.

I had been to Cancun many times before, and always felt sorry for the Mexicans. It didn't matter how much they tried to improve their airport, they were always deluged with tourists arriving from all corners of the world. I fought my way to the rental counter of Air-Cangrejo.

"[Here is your contract. Walk outside and take the Air-Cangrejo's shuttle to our hangar.]"

I got on the shuttle and sat down. In rapid succession, I looked twice at the guy sitting beside me. He must have noticed my expression of disbelief because he said, "[How are you doing Senor Tellez?]"

"[Ramon! What are you doing here?]"

"[I knew you were coming. So I decided to wait for you, before continuing in my way to Chichen Itza.]"

"[Listen, I'd like to thank you for saving my life. I appreciate very much what you did for me.]"

"[Glad to do it. I'm happy for it, but it's part of my job.]"

"[What job? What do you do?]"

"[I work for Jacinto.]"

"[You know what? I just rented an LF jet to go to see Jacinto in Chichen Itza. But I don't have an appointment with him, and he doesn't know I'm coming.]"

"[Don't worry senor, Jacinto is waiting for you. In fact, I'm supposed to take you there,]" explained Ramon.

"[Really? So, you will ride with me.]"

"[Yes.]"

Ramon led me inside Jacinto's shed, an small structure strategically located on the edge of the Cenote. Jacinto wasn't there, and it was very hot and humid. I looked down toward the Cenote's green waters. It was so still that it looked unreal. I wasn't sure that it was really water. I imagined myself jumping into the water to try to find out what it was. I felt terribly depressed and insecure. I turned around looking for Ramon; instead I saw the figure of an old man standing behind me. He appeared to be ethereal, not a real person, like the silhouette of my imagination. I must have fainted because I cannot recall what happened after that. The first thing I remember was seeing Ramon beside me. He asked: "[Senor, senor...how do you feel? Jacinto is here.]"

"[I feel kind of dizzy. What happened to me?]"

"[You looked down into the green water,]" said an old man, who also was standing beside me.

"[Yes, but how do you know?]"

"[I am Jacinto. I know all about that water.]"

I tried to stand up, but Jacinto prevented me from doing it. He then said, "[You better lie flat on the floor for a little longer.]"

A few minutes later, I was up and talking with Jacinto in English. "I heard that this is the only magnetic eye on our planet."

"Yes, the only one left."

"Do you mean there were more than one in the past?"

"Exactly."

"Where?"

"Inside the Great Pyramid of Khufu, in Egypt."

"But that Pyramid is still standing, it's been there for almost five thousand years."

"Yes, but its magnetic eye vanished 722 years before Christ."

"How come? What happened?"

I noticed a change in Jacinto's demeanor. He was more receptive to my questions, and his deep set eyes glowed with enthusiasm.

Jacinto gestured for me to sit on a large rock. Then, he sat close to me on another rock. He said, "Initially, the Egyptian pyramids were Mastabas, funerary monuments erected on top of large tombs. But 2680 years before Christ something extraordinary happened at Giza. A giant complex of three huge pyramids sprouted out of the desert. Nobody knew why they were there or who built them.

"Khufu, a powerful Egyptian pharaoh, ordered the erection of a mortuary temple near the huge pyramids. Thousands of slaves worked in the construction project. Many of them tried to escape, and most of them died in the attempt. A few, most of them Semites, driven by panic and desperation, found deep inside the largest pyramid a secret, and a very well disguised passage. It gave them access to a very special chamber, a place where time didn't exist. There was only space inside the chamber. The Egyptian pharaohs never learned about this extraordinary place. They were holders of absolute power, and never mixed with their subjects. The pharaohs ruled by terror, and in their kingdoms the information traveled in only one direction: from the pharaoh down to the subjugated masses. Many generation of pharaohs used the pyramids exclusively as funerary monuments, for them and their closest relatives.

"But the secret lived among the slaves, and oddly enough some of them lived extremely long lives. Some were Hebrews. In the year 722 B.C., the northern kingdom of the Hebrews, Israel was under the unrelenting attack of the Assyrians. All ten tribes of Israel were conquered by the Assyrians, who carried the enslaved Israelites to Assyria in western Asia. All the Hebrews of the northern kingdom were subjugated, except for the most resolute members of each tribe. These were the ones who could not be broken—Israelites who would rather die than surrender. They formed a band of desperados who faced extermination. As a last resort, they rushed toward the magnetic eye inside the Great Pyramid of Khufu. They disappeared in the green space of space-time without time. After they entered, space-time unwarped and the magnetic eye vanished."

I was amazed by Jacinto's revelations, but when he mentioned 'unwarped space-time' it triggered an spark inside my engineer's mind. I asked, "What exactly is a magnetic eye?"

"The name magnetic eye was improperly coined in the 19th century A.D. by British archeologists who were excavating near the Great Pyramid of Khufu. Electromagnetism was then in the frontier of scientific knowledge. The great scientific minds of the era, Ampere, Faraday, Henry, and Oersted were working hard to unravel its mystery and explain its nature. The British archeologists noticed some inexplicable phenomena around the great pyramid. So, they used their 'avant-garde' knowledge to describe them.

"In reality the small distortion of the Earth's magnetic field around the magnetic eye is only a secondary effect. Early in the 20th century A.D., Einstein established space-time as a four dimensional space in which time and ordinary space are irreversibly combined. He concluded that contrary to our common experience, space and time are not independent of each other. For him there was not space without time and no time without space. But he failed to conceive a crucial characteristic of space-time, which is that in a time-warped space-time, time becomes independent of space, and separated from it. Actually, the real component of time is the only one that disappears from the time-warped domain. The imaginary component of time remains attached to the time-warped domain.

"The space-time inside the Sacred Cenote in Chichen Itza is time-warped and therefore it doesn't contain time. It is a green hole without real time. Therefore, when our friend Ramon jumps into the Cenote, time doesn't pass for him. He only ages when he's outside the Cenote. And that is why he has lived more than a thousand years."

"How about you, how old are you?"

"I am one of the original Israelites that found shelter inside Khufu's magnetic eye," Jacinto said.

"Holly cow! You are almost 3,000 years old! How many Jews gained access to Khufu's magnetic eye?"

"Two hundred twenty-six, including women and children."

"Are they all alive?"

"No, many of them abandoned the magnetic eye when we resurfaced here in Chichen Itza. They mixed with the Indian population of the Yucatan peninsula and Central America."

" What are you saying? Are the Mexicans Jews?"

"Mexico is a big country, but definitely they have a small portion of Jewish blood in them. You must realize that back then the Israelites didn't have the concept of a Jewish race as they have now."

I was astonished, my mind was spinning. Jacinto's revelations were indeed revolutionary. They changed not only my concepts of space and time, but also the image of myself.

"How did you arrive in Chichen Itza?" I asked.

"I don't have a clue. At the time, we didn't realize that we had moved. It was a big surprise when we finally resurfaced in Chichen Itza."

"Aren't you bored? How could you live for so long inside the Magnetic Eye?"

"On the contrary, I'm very happy living here. In fact, inside the Magnetic Eye, science and logic are the rulers. Everything can be explained, and there is not a beginning or an end. Remember, time doesn't exist inside the eye. We see the outside world as a chaotic world, which is rapidly coming to an end."

"No! You can't be right. Why?"

"Because a huge cosmic rock, eleven miles across, is on a collision course with the planet Earth. This asteroid had been in orbit around the sun for billions of years. It never collided with Earth, but its extremely eccentric orbit intercepts the Earth's orbit every 4,666 years. It's a fragment of one of the original moons of Uranus which in the infancy of the solar system collided with a planet-sized object. This cataclysmic impact knocked Uranus on its side and rearranged its system of moons. Fifteen of them remained as Uranus' satellites, with the peculiarity that their orbits are perpendicular to the orbital plane of the solar system's planets. Two of the original moons of Uranus, however, escaped Uranus' gravitational attraction, and crashed with Saturn. A third one was destroyed by the huge impact and one of its pieces became the asteroid that now threatens the planet Earth.

"On the year 2523 B.C., ancient Egyptians were mesmerized by a bright trail of light across the night sky which outshone all the stars and the moon combined. It happened when a huge asteroid glanced off the upper layers of Earth's atmosphere. Full of wonder and reverence, they named it the 'Golden Phoenix.' They predicted that like its namesake, the mythological bird, it would return. They were right. The Golden Phoenix will be here in 2143 A.D. We have 66 years left before collision!"

"Is that why you need our help?" I asked.

"Yes, the United States must shoot down the Golden Phoenix before it hits Earth. If it's not intercepted, our planet will be incinerated; it would be the end of human kind."

"How I can help?"

"You must convince the leaders of every political party that the Golden Phoenix is coming back, that it will be here in sixty six years. And that immediately they should start a project to shoot it down in outer space, or cause it to deviate from its present course."

"What about the other nations? They should be involved in

the project, too."

"Yes, but you should concentrate on the United States. Don't worry, we will take care of all the other nations. You aren't our only guest. In fact, we are working with people from every major country."

"What else do you know about the Golden Phoenix?"

"What more do you want to know about?"

"Anything that could help us track it down."

Jacinto must have sensed that I was willing to cooperate as much as I could with him. He abandoned his usual demeanor of humility and calmness, and became openly enthusiastic.

"I have five critical pieces of information for you," he replied. "The Golden Phoenix has an elliptical orbit around the sun which is almost perpendicular to the plane of the Earth's orbit. The orbital period lasts 4,666 years. It travels at 74,800 miles per hour in the vicinity of the Earth. The last time the Golden Phoenix approached Earth, it passed between the Moon and Earth. Luckily, the sun was on the same side as the Moon was."

"How could you know that if the Israelites entered the magnetic eye in 722 B.C."

"Yes, but don't forget that Semite slaves discovered Khufu's magnetic eye around 2600 B.C. They were the ones that recorded the heavenly event. They thought that the Golden Phoenix was in reality Satan's revenge. That the Devil was planning to annihilate the entire human race, God's creation. The Semite slaves were extremely clever, because they made their naked eye observations with reference to the pyramid's triangular sides and the apex. Later on, throughout time, we consulted with the best minds that the human species had produced, among them Hipparchus, the great Greek astronomer; Euclid, the great geometrician and founder of the Alexandrian School of Mathematicians in Egypt, who used the recorded Semites' observations to determined with great precision the position of the heavenly bodies when the Golden Phoenix almost hit earth; Thycho Brahe, who identified Venus in the Semites' records; Johannes Kepler, and Galileo Galilei who calculated the orbit of the Golden Phoenix; Isaac Newton, who computed the orbital time, the mass, and size of the Golden Phoenix; Albert Einstein, who verified Newton's calculations and resolved errors introduced by the usage of different calendars in different eras. He pointed out that the old lunisolar calendar of the Hebrews was different from the early Mayan calendar which was based on the period of the planet Venus.

"These giants of human intellect could perform this amazing analytical investigation because they knew the position of all the major heavenly bodies with reference to Khufu's Pyramid on the day of the event. Even the position of Venus."

"I'm really impressed. Now it makes sense."

"Are you willing to participate in this crusade to save our planet?" Jacinto asked.

"How can I refuse?"

"Just say no."

"What happens if I don't succeed?"

"Don't worry, you'll succeed. It's written on the timeless wall. That's why we chose you."

"Why me?"

"I don't know."

In silence, Ramon came into the room, grabbed a water bucket which hung in the middle of the room over a pile of hot rocks, and went outside. A couple of minutes later, he returned with the bucket full of water and hung it back up. He caught Jacinto's eye for a second and left.

"Did he refill it with water from the Cenote?"

Jacinto hesitated, then replied, "Yes."

"What will happen if I jump into the Cenote?"

"Please, don't do it! You will not come out on time."

"How many of you did you say you were?"

"Two hundred twenty-six Israelites. A few more than the number of Spaniards that came with the first expedition of Hernan Cortes in 1518."

"Son of a gun. You are always a step ahead of me. Goodbye, my friend."

"Vaya con Dios, amigo," said Jacinto.

The information Jacinto passed on to me was vital for the entire human race. I thought about it, and convinced myself I must take action immediately. That evening I called Marta. "Dear, listen. I learned something extremely important today."

"Did you find Ramon?"

"Yes, he is fine."

"What's the problem now?"

"I can't explain it to you over the phone. All I can say is that Jacinto blew my mind. What he told me is incredible, bigger that anything you can image."

"Oh, sure, same old thing. You're always entangled in the middle of a super secret intrigue."

"My love, you must trust me, I'm not making it up. I need your understanding in this moment of crisis."

"Is your girlfriend there with you?"

"No! What girlfriend are you talking about?"

"Jenny."

"You're talking nonsense. I called to tell you that tomorrow morning I'm flying directly to Washington instead of San Antonio. I must tell Senator Santamarina about my meeting with Jacinto. I'll come back home as soon as I can. I miss you, my darling."

"I miss you too. Bye bye."

10 The Project

Washington D.C.

Senator Luis Santamarina's Office

Monday, 9:48 A.M., 7 June 2077.

"Tito, I believe your story, because I know that you are a very reliable and logical man. We've known each other since elementary school—you aren't a liar. But who else is going to believe that story?"

"I don't know, but I totally disagree with you. In fact, I think, it should be easy to gain the unconditional support of the government and the people of our country. After all, everyone will be affected the same way by The Golden Phoenix. Remember, if it hits our planet, it will annihilate the entire human species."

"Come on, a three thousand year old man? No way, Jose. News reporters will laugh at you."

"I tell you what, get me an appointment with the Administrator of NASA and let him be the judge."

"That I can do. When do you want to have the meeting?"

"As soon as possible."

"I'd take care of that. I'll let you know."

Washington D.C.
NASA Headquarters
Tuesday, 9:05 A.M., 8 June 2077

We stepped off the elevator on the nineteenth floor. The pretty young lady escorting us stopped for a second and, pointing to an exhibit on the other side of the elevator's lobby, she said, "That is the model of the base we plan to build on Mars."

"Yeah, I've seen it before," Luis retorted, smiling and showing no interest in the imposing display.

We turned right toward a set of glass doors on the south side of the building. The left leaf was beautifully decorated with the blue NASA emblem. A sign on the right leaf read: Dr. Jack Goldstein, Administrator.

Once inside the reception foyer, we went directly to the appointment desk, attended by a stunning lady.

"Good morning, Senator."

"Good morning, Margaret."

"Jack will see you immediately."

Jack's secretary came out and led us to his office, which occupied the entire southeast corner of the nineteenth floor. The office of his "Royal Highness," the Administrator of the National Aeronautics and Space Administration, was large and elegantly decorated, yet warm and personal. The furniture was white and dark blue, the carpet was thick, braided white wool, and his desk was set at an angle, just off the tinted glass window, on the southeast corner of the room. There was a conversation area close to the east wall of the room, and three curio cabinets were strategically set on the west side of the room. They contained rare mementos and treasures of past space missions, including some miniature holograms.

Jack sat in his plush swivel chair behind his desk. He stood up and came around to greet us. Shaking hands and smiling effusively, he said, “Luis, my good old friend, glad to see you.”

The Senator introduced me, and we all sat on the conversation area.

“Tito believes that a large asteroid is going to hit our planet in the year 2143. I don’t believe his story, so he asked me to arrange a meeting with you.”

“How large an asteroid?” Jack asked.

“Eleven miles across,” I answered

“How do you know that it will collide with Earth in sixty six years?”

I began telling him the Golden Phoenix’s story. But before I could finish, he interrupted me and asked us to follow him to an adjoining conference room. Once there, he called Joseph Szklaruk, who manages the Asteroids and Meteorites Group at the Goddard Space Center, located just outside the Washington’s beltway.

“Joe, I’m here with Senator Santamarina and Tito Tellez. He’s the Chairman of New Era’s National Executive Committee.”

“Yes, sir, I can see them.”

“Tito has an amazing story about a huge asteroid. I’ll let him tell you all about it.”

It took me only five minutes to narrate the principal facts. Joe was astonished and so interested that he requested my permission to record it. Finally, he said, "For many years we heard the rumor about the Golden Phoenix, but we never could verify it. I suspected its existence because we found a reference to it in some of Einstein's old, handwritten notes."

"Are you actually looking for it?"

"No specifically, but the possibility that it might appear at any time is always present in our mind."

"Any suggestions, Joe?" Jack asked.

"Yes. We should try to verify what Newton determined about the size, mass, and the orbital period of the Golden Phoenix. The British can help us, since they have most of Newton's original papers. The Egyptians can help in the verification of Euclid involvement. The Germans can add Kepler's contribution, and the Italians, with Galileo's."

"Agreed. I'll take care of the requests. Anything else?"

"We must decide, as soon as possible, what to do in case we confirm its existence. Are we going to blast it and break it into smaller pieces or are we going to try to change its course? We are talking about a rock that is eleven miles in diameter and that is moving toward the planet Earth at 74,800 miles per hour. We must intercept it one year before collision time, or when it's at six hundred million miles from Earth. It'll be a very difficult task, provided that it's true that the Phoenix's orbit is perpendicular to the orbital plane of the solar system's planets."

"You're right, Joe, but I'd feel much better if we have three lines of defense instead of one. We can't afford to miss it. We must shoot it down before it hits Earth," Jack said.

"I like that idea," the Senator said. "If you decide that the Golden Phoenix is for real, I'd like to know about it immediately."

"Sorry, Luis, but we must inform the President first," Jack said. "He'll carry the ball from there on. That's his job."

"Don't worry he'll come to us. He's going to need a lot of money," Luis retorted.

"To accomplish this mission, we may need a new class of space crafts. They must be larger and faster than anything we have now," Joe argued.

"And they must be fighter spaceships," Jack added. "I'm sure the armed services are going to get involved in this mission. This is the biggest threat our planet has ever had."

"We have to keep this quiet. We don't want to alarm the public unnecessarily. The story must be verified before releasing it to the media," the Senator said.

"I agree, but I intend to brief the President. The risk is too high to keep it from him," Jack said.

The meeting came to an end. I took the opportunity to ask, "Joe, are you related to David Szklaruk?"

"He was my grandfather."

"Really? You know that he played a very important role in transforming New Era into the largest political party of our country."

"Yes, I'm very proud of him. Floridians elected him three times to the U.S. Senate," Joe said. "Did you know that he died in Cancun?"

"What he was doing there?"

"Mostly enjoying life, but he also got involved in some kind of jewelry business."

On our way out of the building, Luis told me to let NASA handle the problem of the Golden Phoenix and that I should concentrate on my job. He advised me to put all my efforts into trying to keep Texas in the union.

I knew that without Luis' support, I couldn't maintain my position within the party's organization. After the meeting I went directly to National Airport, and took the two o'clock shuttle to New York.

I was getting ready to leave for the building's gym when HK alerted me that I had an incoming call.

"Who's calling?"

"Jenny Douglas ."

"Put her on."

"Tito, my love, I've been trying to get in touch with you for several days."

"Sorry, honey. I'd been very busy."

"Sweetie, I'd problems with Bob."

"Who's Bob?"

"My husband. I don't want to stay with him any longer. He's a bad person."

"Did he abuse you?"

"No yet, but he's always threatening me with isolation and physical punishment if I don't collaborate."

"Collaborate...what do you mean?"

"He wants me to participate in his activities. He's an

strange man with bizarre beliefs. His friends are fanatics or gangsters. Actually, he wants to enroll me in a cult."

"Really...what cult?"

"I don't know and I don't care. They are disgusting. There is something else that you should know."

"What?"

"Oftentimes, when a drug cartel or the Mafia wants to get rid of one of their members, because he's become a liability, they hire Bob to defend him. They know he'll lose the case."

"How can you be married to a person like that?"

"I can't. I want a divorce. Will you help me?"

"Of course. You can count with me for anything. But tell me, does he loves you?"

"Not anymore. I think he's afraid of what I know about him."

"What?"

"If a member tries to leave the cult they put him or her in isolation and counseling. Which is nothing else but intimidation and punishment."

"Jenny, my darling, don't be afraid anymore, I'll protect you with my life if necessary. But, I have problems of my own. I just learned something extremely important in Cancun. The human species is in danger of extinction."

"Honey, what are you saying?"

"My darling, I love you with passion, but I can't tell you any more. Can you hang in there for a little longer?"

"Sure, my love. I'll be waiting for you."

"You know my cellular phone number. If you need me, call at any time."

"Thank you, my love. Don't worry about me, I'll be okay."

That night, I explained to Rafi, my colleague and roommate, that I felt overwhelmed and entangled by the many problems I was suppose to solve.

"You have too many problems," said Rafi. "Do you realize that on one hand you're suppose to save the United States from splitting apart and, on the other hand, you're suppose to save our planet? All that while you're in the middle of a romantic affair with a married and younger lady."

"It's too much." I said.

"You got that right!" Rafi shook his head. "It's too much for any person, dead or alive."

"I wasn't looking for these problems."

"That isn't exactly true," Rafi said. "You knew what you were getting into when you accepted the New Era's job."

"True, but everything else was a total surprise."

"I think that Senator Santamarina is absolutely right. You should let NASA handle the asteroid threat. And you must concentrate in directing our efforts to defeat the Texas' independence referendum."

"I already decided to do that. But what about Jenny, what do I do about her?"

"My friend, you're the only one who can answer that question. Be extremely careful, because that sweet affair could explode in your face and wipe you out completely. No offense, but I think she isn't the right woman for you."

"What do you mean?"

Rafi hesitated for a second; his expression darkened. He shook his head and said, " I hate to say this, but I believe she's an easy woman, a sexual freak."

"You're completely wrong! She's an excellent person, a compassionate person, incapable of hurting anyone. She's full of life. It's delightful to be around her. Besides, it's none of your business."

"Wait a minute, pal...you asked me about her...remember?"

"Oh. Shut your mouth."

Manhattan, New York City
The secure meeting room in New Era's Office
Wednesday, 9:32 A.M., 9 June 2077

Our secure meeting room doesn't have windows or electronic equipment of any kind. Before entering, meeting participants are supposed to leave all their belongings outside. They are screened before entering or leaving the room by our security people, most of them mentally retarded paranoids. I don't control these despotic tyrants. They are contracted and paid for by the San Antonio office, where the headquarters of the party is. The room is cool, bare, and impersonal, but it is indispensable.

The six people attending the staff meeting were trusted party hands. I said:

"Good morning, gentlemen. I invited my friend Ruben Vargas to attend this meeting. He works in the San Antonio office. Last Friday, as all of you know, the Texas governor was assassinated on the front steps of the U.S. Capitol in Washington, D.C. The FBI believes that the perpetrator is somebody connected with the ultra right movement in Texas. But the FBI doesn't have yet any concrete evidence of that. Up to now, we have been considering the ultra right as our allies in the struggle to defeat the Texas independence referendum. Ruben brings us the latest position of our party in this matter."

"Thank you, Tito. The New Era elected leadership met this past Monday in San Antonio. Present were the entire New Era's congressional delegation plus the governors of Arizona, California, Colorado, Florida, Illinois, New Jersey, and New Mexico. They established the following guidelines: The party believes that the ultra right will vote against the Texas' independence referendum regardless of anything we say or do. Don't accept the support of any member of the ultra right. Don't attend any rally or any other political activity to promote the election of any member of the ultra right. If it isn't absolutely necessary, don't attack their point of views. But make it very clear that we don't approved their tactics and methods, and that our political philosophy and goals are completely different from theirs."

Christina, one of the staffers, said, "You keep talking about our party relationship with the ultra right movement in this country, but there are many other issues that are more important to the voters."

Ruben responded, "Indeed, you all know that our candidates are free to choose their own issues—they can differ significantly in their opinions from the party line. However, the basic tenets that make our party so attractive, not only to Hispanics, but to so many other people from all different ethnic groups, haven't changed.

"The Government can't force anyone to speak a specific language.

"The Government can't force anyone not to smoke or drink.

"Tax rate on liquor or tobacco products can't be different from the general sales' tax rate.

"The Government can't apply adult laws and court procedures to minors. It doesn't matter how heinous the crime. And, we believe that the laws and procedures applicable to minors must be overhauled.

"The age of adulthood must be the same for all the states and must apply to all privileges, obligations and penalties.

"Cloning can't be prohibited. But any clone creation procedure must be reported ahead of time. All clones must be registered. Criminals can't be cloned.

"Cyborgs are citizens, robots are not.

"Media reporters must pay for answers! Answers should be copyright protected."

I noticed Christina wiggle inside her cute low cut dress, the latest fashion in office attire for young women. Talking fast and emphatically she said, "There are many other issues that are very popular among the young voters."

"Can you be more specific?" Ruben asked.

Christina took a sip of her herbal tea, leaned back in the chair, and said, "Many people are in favor of changing the laws and amending the constitution to allow the introduction in court procedures not only of the proven facts, but of what's the expected behavior of any citizen according to his or her profile. I'm talking about of a wide range of reprehensible behaviors, like rape, child abuse, spouse abuse, sexual depravation, alcoholism, drug addiction, and many other type of crimes that we know run in families."

"I recognize the need to bring our constitution in line with present days social diseases. But tagging a citizen with a family profile is an extreme idea that has some merits but a lot of drawbacks. That issue is very controversial and our party is not ready to take a position on it yet. Any other questions? Okay, let's go back to work," Ruben said.

Ruben and I went back to my office. I said, "The Mexican President rejected the proposal to incorporate Texas into Mexico."

Ruben sat down and put his feet on my desk. He said, "Excellent. Now our only problem is to defeat the Texas independence referendum."

"That isn't going to be easy. They now have the support of the annexation's proponents; they see Texas independence as a necessary first step. And the Governor's assassination didn't help, either," I said.

"You know what? The FBI found a tiny microprocessor chip lying on the ground, close to the left rear door of the Governor's limousine. They traced the microprocessor chip to a New York wholesaler. The bad news is that he sold millions of them. The FBI believes the hit was carried out by two Cyborgs."

"Master Tito, you have an audio only call," interrupted my office's computer.

"Who's calling?"

"The President of the United States."

"Put him on."

“Mr. Ernesto Tellez?”

“Yes,” I answered, my heart pumping hard and my brain paralyzed.

“Hold for the President, please.”

“Mr. Tellez, this morning Dr. Goldstein briefed me about a meeting that he had with you yesterday. I’d like to see you in person tomorrow. Are you available?”

“Of course, Mr. President.”

“Good. Please stay on the line for the appointment desk. I’ll see you tomorrow. Thank you.”

11 Why me?

I was concerned about the consequences of a meeting with the President. I didn't know how my New Era colleagues would react, especially since I wasn't supposed to reveal the Golden Phoenix story to anyone. I called Senator Santamarina. "Senator the President phoned me this morning."

"I knew that was going to happen. What are you going to do?"

"He wants to see me and I couldn't possibly say no to the President. I'm supposed to meet with him tomorrow morning at eleven o'clock at the White House."

"I understand, but very few other people will. Remember, they know nothing about the Golden Phoenix. The executive committee might demand your resignation."

"Maybe—what can I do? I must convince the President that the threat of the Golden Phoenix is for real. That's number one priority in my book."

"I guess you're right. Be prepared to resign, because you can't reveal your encounter with Jacinto. And you can't tell the people anything about the doomsday asteroid either. It would trigger chaos around the world."

The White House's appointment desk had given me the following instructions:

Don't bring your car to the White House. There isn't parking space.

Be at the main entrance, on the North front of the house, at 10:30 A.M. Tell the guards that you have an appointment (don't say with who) at eleven o'clock. Have your state issued identification card ready.

Don't bring any weapons. They will search you completely before allowing you to go to the next step.

Don't bring computers, telephones, or recording devices, of any type. They will be temporarily confiscated, and sometimes they get lost in the red tape.

Early in the morning of June 10, I rode the rapid transit train from New York city to Union Station in downtown Washington D.C. Once there I caught a taxi to the White House.

A Secret Service agent placed my identification card inside an I.D. card reader, and said: "Please, Mr. Tellez, place your right-hand thumb on the square."

The agent focused on his computer screen. He nodded and keyed in an instruction. A minute later he handed me a barcoded, red visitor pass and told me to clip it on my jacket. He said, "The pass allows you to go to the Central Security Station, the one inside the building." He pointed to a red brick trail. "Follow it to the Central Security Station."

The Central Security Station was part of the executive offices in the West Wing of the White House. The entrance to the West Wing was guarded by two Marines who snapped a military salute as I approached their duty station. Once in the building, I entered the reception foyer where I encountered a metal detector station. I tripped off the alarm when I went through the gate. A big Secret Service agent, who looked like a Washington Redskins lineman with a neck thicker than his head, asked me to empty my pockets and remove my belt, my wrist watch, even my wedding ring. Carefully, he swept me with his hand-held detector. He then asked to see my pass and my personal I.D. card. Distrustfully, with burning eyes, he said, "How come you tripped off the alarm, are you some kind of Cyborg or a bastard Clone?"

The mean-looking man, his firm voice, and his unfriendly presence, immediately reminded me of my days in the Navy. Automatically, I squared my shoulders, adopted an unyielding posture and shouted, "No, sir, I'm not."

The fat-necked agent pointed to a door and commanded, "Go in there."

Pissed off by the nasty Secret Service agent, I had the impulse to punch him in his piggy face, right where his thin lips joined his crooked nose. I imagined him bleeding from his nose, and spitting out his two front teeth. But I reined in my temper. I snatched back my pass and I.D., and walked briskly to the door. Inside the room, I was met by a smiling, friendly-looking man who said, "You almost punched him in the nose, didn't you?"

"Yes, how do you know?"

"I saw your reaction. Our cameras cover the entire area. I'm glad you didn't. Believe me, that cyborg could destroy you in less than ten seconds."

"Is he a cyborg?"

"Sure is. Listen, it's nothing personal, but it is our job. We are responsible for the security of our President."

"Now what?"

"Follow me."

We came to a heavy, metal door. He opened it, saying, "We are going to take X-rays, while you run throughout that narrow corridor."

"Wait a minute. How long I am going to be exposed to X-rays?"

"For less than two milliseconds. Don't worry, it wouldn't harm you."

Reluctantly, I sprinted through the corridor. I pushed the exit door and bumped into a beautiful young lady, who was waiting for me.

"Beg your pardon, miss."

"This way, Mr. Tellez." We walked a few steps to her desk.

"Please, sit down. Let me have the red pass."

I handed it to her, then she handed me another pass, white this time.

"This is your new pass. Wait here until somebody from the President's security detachment comes and escorts you to the President's office." She smiled. "It'll just be a few minutes."

A high class, Ivy League type young lady came to escort me. She was cool and correct but at the same time cordial. By the time we reached the Presidential appointment desk, I'd begun to relax. The desk was attended by two secretaries. I signed in on the President's appointment book. A minute later the

President's secretary came out and led me to the President's office. Two Marines were guarding the access door to the Oval Office. They snapped a military salute as we approached, and one of them opened the door for me.

"Please come in, Mr. Tellez."

I flashed my best smile and approached the desk of the President. He stood up and extended his right hand to greet me. We shook hands.

"Is an honor to meet you, Mr. President."

"Nice to meet you, Mr. Tellez. Please sit down. The story that Jack told me is so far out that I have trouble believing it. So, let's hear it again from the horse's mouth."

"Before I tell you, I want you to know that it doesn't have anything to do with politics."

"I understand, and I believe that you wouldn't lie to me in this matter. My only concern is your mental state. I want to be sure that you aren't an idiot, or that somehow you haven't been brainwashed."

"I'm not insane, Mr. President. I'm sound of mind and capable of rational thinking. I intend to convey to you the facts as I saw them."

I spent the next twenty minutes describing, in great detail, my trip to Cancun and the meeting with Jacinto. He listened raptly to every detail of my story. After I finished, he remained silent for a short while. Then he said, "I know President Carvajal very well. He's my personal friend. I'm going to ask for his permission to explore the Sacred Cenote."

"I don't think he's going to allow that," I said.

The President didn't like my comment. He stared at me. "I

have to try this approach. I'm going to call him right now."

I didn't like his pretense of infallibility. Who did he think he was? The Pope?

"OVO computer call President Carvajal in Mexico City," commanded the President.

"*Marco, mi amigo!* Glad you called. There's something I want to discuss with you," Pedro Carvajal, the Mexican president said.

"Peter, we are planing to explore the Sacred Cenote in Chichen Itza, and I need your consent and authorization," Mark Endicott, the U.S. President declared.

"I'm sorry, my friend, but I won't allow that."

"How come?"

"Would you allow me to explore the Lincoln Memorial or the Washington obelisk?"

"Of course not. They are part of our national heritage. They are sacred to us."

"You don't know this, but the Sacred Cenote is really sacred. It's been there since time immemorial. It's the Holy Grail of the Mayan civilization. In any case, only an Itzae can grant that authorization."

"Come on, Peter. Do you really believe in Itzaes?"

"I do, and you will too, before this is over."

"What?"

"The Golden Phoenix threat."

"Ah, you know about it."

"*Si, mi amigo.* Actually, way before you did. Not only that, the British Prime Minister requested the same thing three hours ago."

"Peter, my friend, please, don't disclose this matter to the press. I need to have a plan of actions before pandemonium breaks loose."

"You can count with my silence, Mark. I'm in the same boat you are. But we can't withhold information from the public indefinitely. Sooner or later, the media will grab hold of the news. So, we don't have too much time left. Whatever you're going to do, do it fast."

"Let's keep in touch, Peter."

After the OVO computer shut off the communication, the President turned to me. "You know what, Mr. Tellez? You were right."

"Glad to be helpful."

"I have a proposition for you. How would you like to work for the Government?"

"As you know, Mr. President, I'm the Chairman of New Era's National Executive Committee. From our office in New York we manage and direct all the party activities in the country. And I believe that because I'm having this meeting with you, I'll be forced to resign. The only person, besides us, who knows the reason for this meeting is Senator Santamarina. What position are you offering to me?"

"If NASA confirms the Golden Phoenix's threat, I need you, and your connection with the Itzaes. I'll create a position to match your excellent technical credentials and your proven managerial skills. I want you to be the head of the agency in charge of planning and coordinating the Government efforts to destroy the Golden Phoenix."

"Thank you, Mr. President. I'd like that position very

much. It'd be a dream come true for me. But I can't accept your offer until I resign my position with New Era. I want to explain to my party leadership the reason for my resignation, and I can't do that until the coming of the Golden Phoenix is officially announced or somehow the media discover the secret.

"Another thing: if the media asks me about this meeting, I will tell them that it was in relation to the Texas referendum. Is that okay with you?"

"I understand your problems. Let's put my offer in hold until NASA confirms the existence of the Golden Phoenix. Your justification for having this meeting is excellent."

"Thank you for your understanding and flexibility."

"Let me know when you're ready. I'll have my staff issue a press release."

"You can count with my loyalty and full cooperation, Mr. President."

"Call me Mark."

"You honor me. My friends call me Tito and I would be delighted if you do so."

"Good bye, Tito."

On my way out of the Oval Office, feeling ten feet tall, I replied, "Good bye, Mark."

As I left the White House, it hit me. Instantly. I knew why me.

12 The Assassins

When I arrived home, on Thursday evening, I was emotionally drained and very tired after the many crucial meetings that I attended during the second week of June, 2077. I was looking forward to a cool drink and an easy conversation with my wife. Marta fixed a couple of Margaritas, and we sat down to drink and talk. I recounted to my wife, in minute details, my encounter with Jacinto and told her all about my meetings with Senator Santamarina, Jack Goldstein, and the President. But I told her nothing about the Golden Phoenix threat. I was afraid that she would tell her sister and the entire world would learn all about the Golden Phoenix the next day. She congratulated me, but she was not too enthusiastic with the President's offer. She couldn't understand why the President wanted me to work for NASA.

Marta was in a receptive mood; I decided to try to iron out our problems. "Dear, after twenty four years of marriage, we should have a very stable and loving relationship. I don't see any reason why we should quarrel so much with each other. We're financially secure, and all our children are totally independent. We're lucky. They are excellent people and good citizens."

"The problem is that you cut me off from your bank account. You're a miserable son of a bitch."

"You were the one that demanded to have an independent bank account," I responded. "You went ahead and separated all your money from mine. I don't have access to any of your accounts. Your money is only yours, and mine is still yours and mine. I put all the money I make into this house, and I've taken you around the world. We're always visiting exotic places, and we go to the most expensive resorts on the planet. We live in the most exclusive building complex in San Antonio. We own a condo in Fort Lauderdale, and a rustic cabin overlooking the Columbia River Gorge. You know very well that money isn't important to me.

"Marta, I'm willing to forgive and forget, and start fresh from the beginning, as we were twenty years ago. If only you promise to respect me. I can't tolerate any longer your insults and your verbal abuses."

"This is your last chance. If it doesn't work out, I'm going to tell my lawyer to start the divorce proceedings," Marta said.

Suddenly the computer interrupted our conversation, "*Master Tito, sorry to interrupt you, but I have an emergency call for you.*"

"Who is it?"

"Ruben."

"Okay, put him on."

"Tito, there are a lot of reporters trying to reach you."

"Really? What they want to know?"

"They are asking questions about your meeting with the President. Not only that, some other members of our party want to know what's going on."

"Tell them that we discussed the Texas independence referendum."

"Are you available for a news conference?" Ruben asked.

"Only if it's absolutely necessary. I'll leave that to your discretion, my friend."

"Is tomorrow okay?"

"Not before seven o'clock in the evening. I'll see you tomorrow."

After the conversation with Ruben, I told Marta, "Whatever you want, my dear, but this is our last chance. You need to cooperate with me, if you want to save our marriage."

Marta finished her second margarita, looked at the empty glass and said, "Tito, my darling, I'll always love you, but something very powerful has pulled us apart. If I die, you know where I want to be buried."

"What are you talking about?"

"I don't know, maybe it's a premonition."

"Don't cry, my darling. Nothing is going to happen to you. We have a long life ahead of us. You're still a young woman. You know what? I bet you'll be the one who will bury me."

She kissed me and looked at me with incredibly tender eyes, as she had never looked to me before. After a while, she said, "I'm going to bed. Are you coming?"

"Of course my love, I always want to be with you."

We had a very tender sex, the kind that you can only have with a beloved wife, in your own bed. It was an unforgettable night. Finally Marta and I had learned to love each other.

Party Headquarters, San Antonio
Ruben's office
9:45 Friday morning.

New Era's headquarters are located at the Central Commercial Complex, in downtown San Antonio. The party rents an entire floor of one of the buildings. I have an office there, which I sometimes use when I stay in San Antonio.

Ruben didn't like my explanation of why I met with the President. He knew that it was an excuse, that something else was going on. He asked, "Do you think I'm mentally retarded? Come on Tito, level with me."

"The only other person that knows about this, besides the President, is Senator Santamarina."

"I figured that because he was the only one in the party that wasn't concern."

"My friend, you need to trust me on this. I can't disclose to you, or to anyone else, what the problem is. However, I can tell you, that it doesn't have anything to do with politics. I'd rather resign my position as Chairman of the National Executive Committee than to jeopardize the lives of millions of people."

"It's that important?"

"Yes."

"Is it somehow connected to Mexico?"

"Not politically. It doesn't have to do anything with Texas, either."

"You lost me, Tito. In fact, I don't want to know anything else about your problems."

"Good...it's better that way. Very smart."

"Master Tito, I have a message from your wife."

“HK, let me have the message on my office computer, I’ll be there in one minute.”

“HK, put her on.”

“Tito, my dear, I need to go to Bayside Marina in Corpus Christi, where my brother keeps his boat. He just called me and said that last night someone broke the starboard side window and entered his boat. According to Pepe, they did substantial damage. He wants me to help him with the police when they come this morning to investigate. Pepe believes that the Satan’s Witness are getting ready to attack him. I’ll be back around one o’clock. I love you.”

“Computer, at what time was this message recorded?”

“At twenty-eight after eight.”

“HK, how many calls did you receive this morning between 8:00 and 8:27.”

“One, at 8:19.”

“Who called?”

“Pepe, your wife’s brother.”

“From where?”

“From the Pelican’s View restaurant in Corpus Christi.”

“HK, call Pepe’s boat.”

“Sorry ,master, that number is disabled.”

“HK, take this message for my wife: Marta, my love, I couldn’t locate you. I’m on my way to Corpus Christi. That place is dangerous. Come home immediately. I’m afraid something terrible will happen. It’s now 10:45 AM. I love you.”

I grabbed “the insurance policy”: an old model 608 Taurus. 357 magnum revolver from my desk’s drawer and returned to Ruben’s office. ”Ruben, how I can get an LF Jet?”

"Go to the roof, look for our takeoff pad, and tell the attendant what you need. I'm sure he knows you."

"Thank you, my friend."

"Anything wrong?"

"I hope not. I'm going to Corpus Christi to bring my wife home. Her brother called her this morning. Someone broke into his boat last night. He believes the Satan's Witness wants to kill him."

"The Satan's Witness! Go, man. Those fanatics are really dangerous. Leave the jerk down there, perhaps you get lucky. Are you carrying a weapon?"

"Yeah, my trusty eight-shot, 357 magnum revolver."

"That weapon is obsolete. Why don't you take a laser gun?"

"They're too heavy and bulky."

I landed at Bayside Marina at 12:15 afternoon. I walked to the marina's office and asked the clerk for directions to the boat.

"Dr. Regalado's boat, Pepe III, is in the eighth berth of the G-pier," replied the clerk.

As I walked to the G-pier, I didn't know what to expect, but my mind was in high gear analyzing all the possibilities. I checked my right trouser pocket, to be sure that my revolver was there. I had never used it before, except for target practice. When my grandfather gave it to me. He said that it was a fine weapon and very unusual because it could fire eight shots without reloading.

As I approached the boat I could hear voices. One of whose

was Marta's voice. I was glad, and for an split second I thought that I'd been an idiot, full of paranoid ideas. I was lucky, nobody noticed my presence when I climbed the boat's ladder. Silently, and with great care, I crawled on the port side walk-around, a narrow passageway between the outside rail and the deck house, toward the forward cabin. Once there, I poked my head up and peeked in through the window. Marta and Pepe were standing up with their back against the navigation console. Two men stood in front of them with their laser guns pointing at them. The bigger one, a fat and repulsive man, carried a huge shoulder-strap, assault laser gun. The smaller one had a hand laser gun. He said, "For the last time, where is Cindy?"

"I don't know where she is, and that's the truth. She was the one who left me. She was having an affair with a Gypsy."

"You're nothing but a fuckin' Chicano. I'll be happy to kill you."

I withdrew my revolver, but before I could shoot it, the guy opened fire and hit Pepe right in the chest. Simultaneously, Marta yelled, "Wait!" He turned around and aimed at her. I shot three times. The impact of the bullets sent him flying against the doorway leading toward the stateroom. He was dead. I became euphoric, and fearless. Meanwhile, his accomplice fired his big gun in my general direction. He missed me, but made a big hole in the wall and vaporized the entire window on the port side of the boat. I ran in the direction of the forward deck. When I was about to pass in front of the enclosed bridge, I heard Marta yelling, "Look out!" I dove toward the starboard side. The guy shot his powerful assault laser gun again. He was an split second late and missed me completely. The sliding door by the helm was wide open, so when I stood up, I saw the assassin still looking toward the forward deck. I fired my magnum three times. On his way down, he fired his gun and blew up a big chunk of the upper deck. Marta rushed toward me at the precise moment that a third assassin who was searching the aft stateroom, fired his gun. He hit Marta in the back. The laser ray bored a hole in her body, and her heart exploded. She fell dead in my arms. I didn't have time for an emotional farewell. The assassin was coming toward me ready to fire his diabolic weapon. But he didn't hurry. He was enjoying the moment. The sarcastic asshole stopped and said, "Stupid! You already fired all your six bullets."

I waved my revolver. "Oh! Gee I forgot." Bang, bang....

He fell dead, a big hole in his forehead, and a large piece of his "smart" brain plastered on the fridge's door.

I picked up Marta's body and held her up. I cried aloud, disconsolately. When the coast guard and the police arrived, it turned out that the fat man was badly hurt but not quite dead.

13 The News Conference

ABEN's news announcer: "This is Robert Miller reporting from New Era's office in San Antonio, Texas. Today at 12:30 P.M., the wife and brother-in-law of Ernesto Tellez, Chairman of New Era's National Executive Committee were assassinated in Corpus Christi, Texas. Mr. and Mrs. Tellez were aboard a yacht owned by Dr. Armando Regalado, Mrs. Tellez's brother, when three members of the Satan's Witness cult carried out the murderous attack. Let's listen to Mr. Ruben Vargas, a New Era spokesman, who is about to make a statement to the Media."

"Mr. Tellez," Ruben said, "asked me to read this statement: Members of the Satan's Witness cult executed my brother-in-law in front of my eyes and were about to execute my wife when I intervened and engaged the murderers in a gun battle. They murdered my wife. I killed two of them and wounded a third. I've described to the police, in great detail, my battle with the Satan's Witnesses. My lawyer, Mr. Benjamin Rosenthal, will represent me concerning this vicious crime perpetrated by the Satan's Witness. The party has accepted my resignation as Chairman of the National Executive Committee. I intend to hold a news conference within one week of my wife's burial. Thank you. Signed, Ernesto Tellez, June 11, 2077."

ABEN's news announcer: "Stay tuned to ABEN for more details about these extraordinary events. We switch now to Corpus Christi, for an interview with Chief Toledano, Corpus Christi police chief."

"This is Pablo Garrido reporting from Bayside Marina in Corpus Christi. Chief Toledano, what really happened here?

"At 7:33, this morning, Dr. Regalado reported that someone had broken into his Sport Cruiser and vandalized it. At 9:17 A.M., members of the Bay Police Department responded to Dr. Regalado's complaint. Their investigation showed that the perpetrators broke the glass window on the starboard side and entered the boat, where they inflicted considerable damage to the navigation equipment and the furniture."

"Chief, who were the perpetrators?"

"The marina security systems provided us with an infrared picture of the perpetrators as they boarded the boat, and we found a blood-stained bandana inside the boat. We believe that one of them was cut as he entered the boat through the broken window. We are comparing the DNA of the blood stain in the bandana with the DNA of the suspects."

"Does the matching apply to all three suspects or only to the one still alive?"

"To all three of them."

"Was Dr. Regalado in the boat when the break-in occurred?"

"No, and we verified his alibi."

"What happen after that?"

"We aren't completely sure, because both Dr. Regalado and his sister are dead. She arrived on the yacht while we were still investigating the break-in. But we have a very detailed statement of Mr. Tellez. It was a voluntary account of the events as he lived through them."

"Is Mr. Tellez a suspect?"

"No. We know that both Dr. Regalado and his sister were killed by the weapons carried by the two dead suspects. We also know that Mr. Tellez was carrying an old explosive type weapon, a 357 magnum revolver. And that is the weapon which killed the two members of the Satan's Witness cult. That proves Dr. Regalado and his sister were killed first."

"Are you going to charge Mr. Tellez?"

"No, he is clearly the victim. He displayed great courage and exceptional valor when he fought a gun battle with three cult enforcers," Chief Toledano turned and got a piece of paper from a police officer. "Someone just handed me a note which says that the DNA found in the bandana's stains matches the DNA of the surviving suspect, the one that is now in the hospital. This indicates that he also participated in the breaking and entering earlier this morning."

"Is he a suspect?

"Yes, of course."

"Does the Coast Guard have jurisdiction in this case?"

"No, we do."

"Chief Toledano, thank you for your comments...We switch back to the network."

After my interview with the police, I wasn't in any condition to fly or drive. I checked myself into a hotel in Corpus Christi. When the rush of adrenaline through my body subsided, my mood changed from ready to fight to depression. I couldn't stay in denial any longer. I realized that Marta was gone forever. I felt alone, abandoned, sorry for myself. I spent a long time looking at the bedroom's ceiling, without noticing its color or finish.

Suddenly, the hotel's computer alerted me that some one was calling me. It was Ruben. He brought me back to reality and helped me draft a statement for the media. Afterward, I called all my three children: Kiki, Arturo, and Rosalyn. They already knew. I shared my ordeal and we cried together.

My oldest son Kiki asked, "Do you know when the Coroner will release Mom's body to us?"

"No, I don't. He doesn't work over the weekend. So, I guess sometime Monday or Tuesday."

"I'll be home later tonight," said Arturo.

"Me, too,"said Rosalyn.

We agreed that I would join them the next morning and

make plans for the funeral.

The news of Marta's assassination and my battle with the Satan's Witness affected Jenny deeply. She was sure that our affair triggered the events that culminated in Marta's death. The day after the assassination, full of remorse and possessed by guilt feelings, Jenny went to see her friend Sharon at her home near the campus of the University of Texas at San Antonio, where Sharon works in the Department of Social Studies.

As she looked deep into her friend eyes, Jenny tried to appear calm and composed, but her wet, glowing eyes indicated that she was in the middle of an emotional calamity.

"I've an oppressive feeling in my heart and a terrible headache. I can't stop thinking about Tito," Jenny let her voice trail off and whispered, "I'm afraid I've lost him forever....He's going to blame me for his wife assassination."

"Maybe not. It takes two to tango," said Sharon. "He is also responsible for everything that happened between you two."

"I flirted with him....Oh God....The Sunday after Tony's funeral, I went back to the school's cafeteria hoping that he'd come back to get his hat."

"I know that. I was there. But he came back on his own. Didn't he?"

Jenny didn't answer. Instead, she lowered her eyes and wiped them off with an overused facial tissue. "I don't want to lose him...I prefer to die."

"Don't feel sorry for yourself. I hate to see you looking so sad."

"What shall I do?"

"The least you can do is go to Marta's funeral. You must offer your condolences to him."

"You think so?"

"Definitely. But you must be discreet."

"His entire family is going to be there....How can I face them?"

"Oh Jesus....Listen if you don't behave and act like a grown up woman, you're going to lose him for sure," said Sharon. "You must show him that you care, that you will do for him anything...embarrassing or not."

"You're right...I'll go. But what do I say?"

"Not too much. Above all, don't put him in an embarrassing situation."

"Sharon, you're an Angel. I treasure your friendship," said Jenny. "Can I stay with you for a couple of days? I don't want to see my husband now."

"Sure, as long as you need," replied Sharon. "Did Bob threaten you?"

"No, but I have a visceral feeling that he master minded the whole thing."

"Really?"

"I don't have any proof, but I think he organized the Satan's Witness attack."

"Why?"

"Revenge. That miserable coward don't have the guts to fight with Tito. So, he used the Satan's Witness to punish Tito and anybody related to him."

Texas 2077

The funeral services for Marta and Pepe were held at St. Francis Catholic Church, on Thursday, June 17, 2077. Leaving church and before I could get into the limousine, I saw Jenny, and she saw me. She didn't tried to talk to me. Later, in the cemetery, I saw her watching the burial ceremony.

Marta was buried at the Southwest Memorial Cemetery in our family plot, next to my mother. Pepe had been divorced for several years, and his marriage to Cindy had been so brief that it didn't even count. He was buried in the Regalado's family plot. I was leaving the burial tent, surrounded by all my children, when Jenny approached me. She said, "I understand your pain, and I am very sorry for your loss."

I didn't want to display any tender feelings toward Jenny. I thought it would dishonor Marta's memory. It was my beloved wife's funeral, and I wanted to show respect and love for her. I wasn't alone—I was a part of our family. I was the husband, surrounded by our children. For me, it was extremely important to convey dignity in my actions. I simply replied, "Thank you."

As we continued toward the limousine, she stayed behind. I didn't look back.

"Who is she?" asked my daughter.

"A friend of mine."

On our way back home, the chauffeur said over the limousine's intercom, "Sir, the President wants to speak with you. He's on channel two. Audio only communication."

"Yes, Mr. President."

"On behalf of my wife and myself, I'd like to extend our deepest sorrow for your loss. Please accept our sincere condolences and sympathy."

Although I knew that the President was a consummate politician, and that he was accustomed to giving condolences, I was moved by his warm statement, delivered with a superb touch of high class.

"Mark," my voice cracked with emotion. "On behalf of the entire Tellez family, I want you to know that we appreciate your condolences very much."

"You're welcome, Tito. And don't worry about anything, because NASA doesn't have an answer yet. But for your information, they are working hard to verify your story."

"Glad to hear that, because I need time to sort things out. Nevertheless, I'm determined, now more than ever, to help as much as I can."

"That's the American spirit. Goodbye, my friend, take care."

Ernesto Tellez's News Conference
New Era's Offices in Downtown San Antonio
Tuesday 2:00 P.M. , June 22, 2077.

I met with Ruben, just before the news conference, to rehearse my answer to reporters' probable questions.

"Don't worry about reporters," said Ruben. "Just tell them what happened. You know the facts better than anybody else."

"I intent to do that, but I'm not in the frame of mind to play politics with sleazy reporters. I might lose my composure if they ask questions based on rumors and innuendoes."

"I don't think they will ask unsubstantiated questions," said Ruben, "They could be severely punished by the National Board of Media Reporters. Unethical reporters can lose their license."

"I know, but I still feel uneasy about this conference."

The building's auditorium was full to capacity. It resembled a bee hive, reverberating with murmur, whisper, and endless chatter. Ruben introduced me to the members of the media. He said, "Gentlemen, as you know on June eleven, Mr. Tellez resigned the chairmanship of the National Executive Committee. He's going to read a brief statement and then he'll take questions. As is our custom, you must pay two thousand dollars for each answer. The money will be donated to the construction fund of St. Francis High School."

I walked to the podium. "The murder of my wife and brother-in-law doesn't have anything to do with Texas' politics," I said. "The Satan's Witness were chasing my brother-in-law. My wife was killed because she witnessed his execution. I had come to her rescue after she left a message in my HK computer telling me where she was going and why.

"In this critical moment in the history of Texas, the New Era party is doing everything it can to keep Texas as part of the United States of America. And that's the most important thing of all. I resigned as Chairman of the National Executive Committee because I didn't want to embarrass the New Era party with the sad details of my personal affairs. I don't want to detract from the party's effort to win the referendum of August 31."

"Mr. Tellez will take questions now," Ruben told reporters congregated in the auditorium.

"Why were the Satan's Witness chasing your brother-in-law?" asked the Corpus Christi Monitor's reporter.

"The Satan's Witness murdered my brother-in-law because they thought that he killed his wife. She was a prominent member of their cult. They considered her to be some kind of Goddess," I answered.

"What happened to her? Where is she?"

"She disappeared three months ago. Dr. Regalado reported that to the police. They couldn't find her, either. He was very much in love with her. She was beautiful."

"Mr. Tellez, what was the subject of your meeting with the President on June ten?" asked the ABEN's Reporter.

"We discussed the Texas referendum. The President is our ally in this struggle."

"Anything from the meeting that you can share with us?"

"No. You'll have to ask the President for that."

"Two days before you met the President, you and Senator Santamarina have a meeting with the NASA Administrator. Why?"

"He's an old friend of Senator Santamarina, and I had some questions regarding the Houston Space Center and about what will happen to it in case the referendum initiative wins."

"Is the Corpus Christi's district attorney going to press charges against you?" asked the Global-TV Network's reporter.

"You'll have to ask him. I don't think he will. Remember I'm one of the victims. In fact, I'm lucky to be alive."

"Was Dr. Regalado a member of the Satan's Witness?"

"For a little while he was, and that's how he met Cindy, his estranged wife. He was a man of wild ideas, but not a killer. And for that he lost his life."

"How long were they married?"

"She abandoned him ten days after the wedding. I understand she was considerable younger than he was."

"How were your relations with your wife?" asked the Fame & Money's reporter.

"Excellent. We had been married for twenty four years, when this happen."

"Sir, we have a picture of you entering the Golden Empire Hotel with a Mrs. Jenny Douglas."

"In my line of work, I meet with many people, male and female. I often go out to lunch or dinner with many of them. I don't see what that has to do with this news conference."

"But it does, sir. Her husband was retained by the Satan's Witness to represent their critically wounded member."

"Really? That doesn't change anything."

I was embarrassed by the indiscreet questions of the prying reporter. I was relieved when Ruben rushed to the podium and said, "Gentlemen, that was the last question. Thank you."

14 Meditation Rock

Overwhelmed by the recent events in my life. I decided to go away for a few days to my favorite retreat, a rustic cabin overlooking the Columbia River Gorge from the Oregon side. It was our vacation home purchased for Marta on our fifth anniversary. We had spent many happy days there with the children, days full of activities and contact with nature. We used to watch wild geese flying back toward their nests on the Washington side of the Columbia River. Precise and single-minded as only birds can be, the geese always spent most of the day in the Oregon's fields. At dusk they would return, flying in perfect V-shaped flocks, honking as they passed over. It was a ritual that enriched our souls.

There, I was sure, I could meditate and gain a spiritual perspective of my life. So, three days after the news conference, on the morning of the twenty-fifth of June, I traveled to Hood River, a town on the western part of the gorge east of Portland. I rented a car at HRI airport and drove straight to my cabin twelve miles to the west. The last time we were there was in January, when Marta and I went downhill skiing at the Mount Hood Ski resort. I spent the rest of the day doing housekeeping. The house was full of memories. As I oiled my mountain bike, I could not avoid crying. I cleaned and oiled her bike too, as if she were there with me. Now that she was gone I forgot about all the bad things that I used to complain about, and remembered only the good times we had together. Our lives were so intertwined, that it was impossible to tear them apart. When she was killed, part of me died with her.

The next day, I decided to go to Meditation Rock, one of the innumerable rock formations, formed millions of years ago by basaltic lava floods that created the world renowned gorge. Meditation Rock is close to the Mosier Twin Tunnels of the Old Columbia River Road, a section of the ancient highway near downtown Hood River.

I crossed the Hood just before it pours into the Columbia and parked my car near Highway 35. I was in the process of taking my bike off the rack on top of the car trunk when somebody behind me called in Spanish, "[Good morning mister Tito.]"

Recognizing the voice, I hesitated for a second before turning around. I shouted, "[Ramon! What are you doing here?]"

"[You always ask the same question,]" affirmed Ramon.

"[Picking pears in Hood River.]"

"[And your reply is always the same,]" I said.

We both laughed while bear hugging each other.

"[Sit down,]" he said, "[I want to talk with you.]"

I sat down on the highway's guard rail. He reclined against my car right door facing me.

"[Listen, I am not good at this, but I want to give you my condolences on the premature deaths of your wife and brother-in-law.]"

"[Thanks. But what are you really doing here?]"

"[Your brother-in-law's wife, Cindy was sent to San Antonio to kill you.]"

"[Who sent her?]"

"[I don't know and I don't want to know,]" replied Ramon.

"[What happened to her?]"

"[I made her an offer that she couldn't refuse.]"

"[Son of gun, so you were the Gypsy with whom she left.]"

"[Yeah...I saved your life.]"

"[Where is she now?]"

"[Gone forever. She wasn't a real person.]"

"[Why then the Satan's Witness killed Marta and Pepe?]"

"[They didn't know who she was. So they assumed Pepe was responsible for her disappearance.]"

"[Did you come all this way to tell me that?]"

"[Partially. But there's another reason. You might be asked to go into the Sacred Cenote and explore it. Don't do it.]"

"[Why not?]"

"[Trust me, you'll never come out of there alive or dead.]"

"[Okay, I'll say no.]"

"[Good.]" said Ramon.

"[Anything new on the Golden Phoenix?]" I asked, "[How come you're so quiet about it?]"

"[We're used to it. We've been trying to fix that problem for thousands of years and we're still working hard on it. That's another reason I'm here.]"

"[Where are you staying?]"

"[Nowhere. I'm leaving in a few minutes.]"

"[What's the rush?]"

"[I told you we're working hard. Goodbye Tito.]"

"[Goodbye Ramon.]"

I watched him walk toward downtown Hood River. Then, I got my bike off the rack and started to ride the three miles ride to Meditation Rock. Once there I climbed fifty feet to the top. While Meditation Rock is not the highest point in that area of the gorge, the view was splendid.

Impressive lava flows were frozen in time, and there were large rock formations on both sides of the gorge. The trees were tall and in this season very green. But what I liked most was the feeling of solitude, which was accentuated by the sound of the wind. Down below the ever present windsurfers "effortlessly" split the frigid waters of the Columbia, reminding me that civilization was still close.

I didn't think about my problems. The place gave me the serenity to think about the important things in life that are sometimes taken for granted and easily forgotten. I recalled the things that make me happy—like outside activities and contemplating nature, eating and drinking what I like in peace without stupid chatter, having a meaningful conversation with somebody you love, giving the correct answer to a child's question, displaying my wit to my friends, of feeling fulfilled when I accomplished a goal. I thought of the heart-warming experience of seeing lust converted into unconditional love. My mind drifted to Jenny and our relationship. On the spur of the moment, I took my helmet and threw it as far as I could. I did the same with my riding gloves and the fresh water bottle.

Two hours later, back in my cabin, I pondered over the political situation. Texas was inexorably tilted toward independence, and that wasn't going to change, no matter what I did. The events were telling me that my life's purpose was not to save Texas, but to help save the planet.

Before departing San Antonio, I had instructed my Home Keeper computer not to let through any call for me without obtaining authorization from the computer at the cabin. I wasn't surprised when the HK cabin computer alerted me that its brother in San Antonio was having a hard time with a persistent caller who wanted to get through to me.

"HK who's calling?"

"Mrs. Jenny Douglas."

I thought for a moment. It was impossible for me to hide from her, because she had my "number." No reason to stay away from Jenny and torture myself while doing it. Suddenly I realized the real reason for my trip to Meditation Rock was not to meditate, but to hide from her. I didn't want to be seen with her only fifteen days after Marta's assassination.

"HK put on the caller."

"She is not on line, but I will get her for you."

Three minutes later I was delighted when I saw Jenny's face on the screen. She always looked honest, accommodating, ready to concede if she was wrong, the complete opposite of Marta, who had never admitted anything and would rather have died than say she was at fault.

"Tito, my love, I've been trying to get in touch with you since this morning. I was worried. How are you doing?"

"I'm okay, but I miss you."

"Tito, I watched your news conference. My darling, you must believe me. I didn't know that my husband, Bob, was the lawyer for the Satan's Witness. I'm embarrassed and ashamed."

"Dear, I understand. You don't need to explain anything. I knew that you were suffering."

"I love being with you. I think about you constantly. I wish we could live together," said Jenny.

"That would be wonderful, but it wouldn't be smart. We have to wait. I'll talk to an attorney friend. Jenny, my love, will you marry me when you're free?"

"Yes! a million times yes. I've loved you since the moment we met at St. Francis."

"Baby...you make me so happy."

"When will you be home?"

"The day after tomorrow. I can't wait to see you. Besides, I need to tell you about something delicate...something you must know before we get married."

15 The Presidential Appointment

July was a wonderful month. It was the eye of the storm. Not since my childhood had I had a period of time so free of responsibilities. I'd been liberated from a bad marriage, and I had no big projects to manage. My relationship with Jenny was full of passion, and we had many romantic encounters. The only thing that prevented it from being perfect was Jenny's husband.

Jenny kept her word. She sued her husband for divorce. And he blamed me for it. His private detectives spoiled some of our romantic encounters. One of them kicked open the door of the hotel at which we were staying in Las Vegas, and took a snapshot of our empty bed. Luckily, he'd been too late; we were in the balcony admiring the view of the "Strip."

I told Jenny everything about the Itzaes, the Golden Phoenix, the interview with the President and what he'd proposed me. She was very receptive and willing to follow me, as she put it, to the ends of the universe.

Wednesday, 4 August 2077, 1:14 P.M., Eastern Time.

ABEN News: "This is Greg Spencer reporting from our studios in New York City. Our latest poll indicates that the Texas' Independence Drive is losing ground. As of today, only fifty-eight percent of the Texans will vote in favor of independence. A two-thirds majority, or sixty seven percent of the voters, is required to win the referendum.

"Professor Ronald Howtorne, of the Center for Long Range Exploration of the Cosmos, disclosed to a reporter at our affiliated station in Tucson, Arizona that the Center was very busy trying to track a huge asteroid said to be on a collision course with Earth. Subsequently, Professor Howtorne read a statement retracting his original revelation, discarding it as baseless speculation. The revelation had opened a proverbial Pandora's box. The Center's communication network is flooded, even as we speak, with inquiries from all corners of the world. Stay tuned to ABEN for more on this extraordinary news. We switch now to our senior correspondent at the White House."

"Good afternoon. This is Chuck Haley reporting to you from Washington D.C. Last night the President met with Jack Goldstein, the NASA administrator, and several members of his cabinet. They briefed the President about a large asteroid that some people claim is on a collision course with our planet. In a statement read just a few minutes ago the White House's Press Secretary disclosed that the U.S. Government isn't totally sure that the Golden Phoenix exists. However, the consequences of being wrong in this problem are so frightful and irreversible that the President is not taking any chances. Until proven otherwise, the Government is assuming that it does exists."

"Chuck, what specific information does the Government have about the asteroid?" Greg, the ABEN announcer, asked.

"The information the White House's Press Secretary provided to the Press is the following:

"The asteroid is eleven miles in diameter.

"It has an orbital period of 4666 years.

"It travels in an extremely eccentric elliptical orbit at 74,800 miles per hour in the vicinity of the Earth.

"The last time it came close to Earth was in the year 2523 B.C. It will be here again in sixty-six years, or in the year 2143 A.D."

"How do they know all this?" Greg asked.

"From observations made back in 2523 B.C. by slaves of the Egyptian pharaoh," Chuck answered.

"Slaves? Did they provide any specific information about these slaves?"

"Yes. They were Semitic people who had been subjugated by an Egyptian pharaoh. Looking for freedom, some of them found refuge in a secret chamber of the Great Pyramid of Khufu."

"Why are we just discovering this now?" Greg asked.

"I don't know. There are many pieces missing from this story. The statement put out by the White House raises more questions that it answers. But the media around the world is working on this news. I expect that we'll have more answers in the next few days."

As soon as I learned about the statement from the White House I called the President. I told him that I was ready to assume the responsibilities of the position that he'd offered to me. He was glad to hear from me, and said that he would announce my appointment in the next few days. He mentioned that someone from his staff would call me to make the proper arrangements for my move to Washington.

Immediately after talking with the President, I called Ruben and recounted the amazing story of the Golden Phoenix. I told him about my encounters with Ramon Linares, about my visit to the Sacred Cenote, and how I met Jacinto, who was a three thousand year old Itzae. It was then that Ruben told me he understood clearly, for the first time, why I met with the President. I asked him to relate the information to the members of New Era's National Executive Committee.

Filled with high expectations, and with a brand new life ahead of me, I went immediately to see Jenny. I wanted to tell her in person about our impending move to Washington, D.C. She was thrilled with the possibilities and the challenge that my new job presented to both of us. She said, "Sweetie, when I met you I never dreamed something like this would happen. But now that it has, I love you more."

"My darling, I feel the same way. I was living a dull life

dedicated to my work. But now, I'm embarking upon a great adventure with you my dearest love. I'm very lucky that I found you. We have so much in common, we are so alike, and you understand me so well, that I enjoy your company immensely."

"Tito, my love, I don't want to be separated from you, not now or ever," Jenny said. "What do we do about the lawyers and my divorce?"

"I don't care anymore. Let's go to Washington, find a place to live and move in together. How does that sound to you?"

She couldn't contain herself any longer. She threw herself into my open arms. I lifted her and swung her around. "I am so happy..."

She couldn't finish her sentence. We started to kiss and spun around like a couple of kids.

Early Monday morning, August 9, we took off for Washington in Jenny's car. On Wednesday, we checked in at the Washington-Beltway Marriott. That night, watching the evening news at the hotel, I learned that the President had announced my appointment during a news conference the day before.

We rented a three bedroom apartment overlooking the Potomac south of Great Falls Park and west of the Beltway. It was a great location not too far away from the District of Columbia, but secluded and remote from Washington's chaotic traffic. I wanted to give Jenny all the room she needed to live comfortably and securely.

On Monday morning, August 16, I called my contact in the Presidential staff. He told me to make all the necessary arrangements to move my furniture to Washington, and then to present the bill when the move had been completed. He told me that my office would be located, temporarily, in the same building that the NASA's national headquarters were, and that they were waiting for me to show up.

"Honey, do you know a dependable moving company?"

"South West Van Lines. They did a good job when we moved to San Antonio seven years ago," replied Jenny.

"Where do you move from?"

"Los Angeles."

I contracted South West Van Lines to pack all my belongings and move most of them to our apartment in Northern Virginia, and to place the rest in storage. I agreed to be in my apartment in San Antonio on Tuesday morning, August 24, the day the movers would come to do the packing. We decided to move only my furniture and leave Jenny's furniture at her home until her divorce was finalized.

16 Big Shot

I was sworn in at the White House on Tuesday, 17 August 2077, by President Endicott. His chief of staff told me that he chose to administer the oath in a combined ceremony with another appointee. It was a brief unannounced ceremony with no fanfare.

Afterward, however, I had a good working session with the President. He said, “Your work isn't going to be easy. The media already knows that you're supposed to coordinate all our efforts to destroy the Golden Phoenix.”

“That's all right as long as they don't discover my connection with the Itzaes.” I sat across from him at the large presidential desk, an exquisite piece of nineteen century furniture.

"Since August 10, when I announced your appointment, they have been investigating you in minute detail. Be very careful with what you say and do. They already know that you went to Cancun right after you witnessed the Texas Governor's assassination. In response to their questions, I told them that I knew nothing about your connection with the time-share salesman. That it was my understanding you met him by pure coincidence. They also are taking a second look at the shootout on your brother-in-law's boat. I suggest that you immediately hire a Media Deputy. He or she must be very sharp and experienced in dealing with the media."

"What is the agency's name, and how big is its budget?"

"It'll be called NATA, for National Asteroid Threat Administration. Officially, however, it isn't an agency yet. It needs congressional approval. But don't worry, it'll be approved, for sure. In the meantime, you'll use NASA's funding. You'll have an initial staff of 35 of NASA's employees."

"I think that a meeting with Jack Goldstein is in order to establish my working parameters," I said.

"Very wise. Go ahead and talk with him. I instructed him to cooperate with you as much as possible. You'll find that he'll please you in everything. Let me know if there's anything you need."

I sensed that the meeting had come to an end. The President could not expend more time with me. "Mark, thank you very much for your support and advice. When do you want me to brief you on our activities?"

"I'll be in touch through my staffers, but be ready for a personal briefing in two weeks. By the way, what happened with the Texas Referendum?"

"It's looking better every day. I believe we're going to win."

"Anything new in your personal life?"

"A lot. I'm engaged to be married. She's twelve years younger than me."

"Congratulations! Can you handle her?"

"I'm trying my best."

"Don't overdo it. Save something for our project."

"Thank you Mark, I appreciate your kindness."

"You're welcome. Good luck."

The news of the approaching asteroid had the potential of producing mass hysteria. In fact, the situation around the White House was deteriorating rapidly. The media scrambled to be in sync with the people's appetite for anything related to the Golden Phoenix. It was the biggest news story ever. People all over the world demanded more information about the Golden Phoenix. They wanted to know the specific place and the exact moment of the impact, and most important, what they could do to survive it. Some wanted to know if it was best to be aboard a ship or in a submarine in the ocean. A million different questions and no answers. To make the things worse, thousands of religious fanatics preached around the clock, proclaiming their own biased interpretation of the approaching disaster.

I used one of the Presidential air shuttles to commute from the White House to NASA's national headquarters. It was the only practical way to get out of the White House. Once in the air, and far away from the commotion surrounding the White House, I ordered a large bouquet of red roses for Jenny.

Jack Goldstein, was waiting for me on the landing pad reserved for the Government Chief Executive Officers. Jack was a very pleasant person who enjoyed doing favors for others. He erected bridges across human's minds, a benevolent human-spider building a web of friends with compatible goals. "Let's go to my office and I'll brief you on what we have done for your agency," he said.

"That's exactly what I had in mind. I appreciate the favor."

In marked contrast with the impression that I'd gotten when Senator Santamarina and I had first visited him, Jack's office was in disarray. Several piles of ancient books and old reports were on top of his desk. Jack said, "Excuse me for the messy room, but since you dropped the big bomb, we had been working long hours with very old information in non-digital format."

"Sorry about that, my friend. I can see that you've been real busy."

"How was your meeting with the President?"

"Fine, I'm real happy with the outcome."

"We cleared twelve thousand square feet, the entire eighth floor, to make room for your agency temporary quarters," Jack said.

"I'd like to see the space. I want to start working as soon as possible."

"Of course, but before we go down there, I'd like to inform

you of what we had accomplished so far."

"I'm all ears."

"We verified Newton's, Kepler's, Galileo's, and Thycho Brahe's calculations and findings about the Golden Phoenix. We're convinced it's true that the Golden Phoenix almost collided with Earth in the year 2523 B.C. We developed a computer model of the of its orbit, and we believe the Golden Phoenix passed at less than one hundred miles from the Earth's surface. The model corroborated all the other data that Jacinto provided to you, with exception of its orbit's angle with reference to the ecliptic plane—the plane of the Earth's orbit. We can't compute the exact angle. Our margin of error is five degrees on either side of the perpendicular to the ecliptic plane. To improve on that result we would need the data from a second observation of the asteroid. It's not realistic to assume that we could get a second set of data, although we might, if we're lucky, detect the Golden Phoenix two years before impact time."

"How far away would it be two years before impact time?"

"A billion miles away."

Jack wanted to provide me with the best available information. Rather than risking any mistake or omission, he suggested we go to the conference room next door and invite NASA's experts on asteroids, Dr. Joe Szklaruk from the Goddard Space Center, and Dr. Bob Patterson from the Ames Research Center in California, both well known astrophysicists and NASA leading scientists in asteroid research.

They joined the meeting through a secured NASA's video network. Jack opened the conference by introducing me to Dr.

Patterson. “Bob, you haven’t met Mr. Tellez. He was appointed by the President to head NATA, the new agency. You and Dr. Szklaruk are going to be working for him.”

“Starting when?” Bob asked.

“It’s effective immediately. The President and the Congress don’t want to waste any time in government red tape. As far as they’re concerned, we are in a state of war against the Golden Phoenix,” Jack said.

“Yes, sir. I’m glad the Government is acting quickly against this threat,” Dr. Patterson said.

“Tito, do you have any questions for them?” Jack asked.

“I do. How important is it to know the exact angle of the Golden Phoenix’s orbit?”

“Extremely important. The more precisely we know its orbit angle with reference to the ecliptic plane, the farther away our spaceships could intercept and destroy the asteroid. If we accept an uncertainty of ten degrees in angular position, we will need to wait until it’s real close, frighteningly close. Of course, everything depends on the number and kind of fighting spaceships that we could launch. For instance, if we launch twenty spaceships, each at a half degree increment, we should be able to contact the asteroid when it’s at one hundred fifteen million miles from us, or eighty days from impact time. That, of course, is not acceptable,” Joe said.

“What do we need to do, to intercept the Golden Phoenix at least one year before impact time?”

“To accomplish that, we must work on three fronts. We must get a second set of observations to compute the exact asteroid’s orbit. We must improve the speed and range of our spaceships. And, finally we must improve the range of the sensors and detectors on board the spaceships. The present day generation of spaceships isn't good enough," Bob said.

"How could we get that second set of observations?" I asked.

"We could launch one thousand unmanned spacecrafts, each at one hundredth of a degree increment within the window of eighty-five to ninety-five degrees. The interception point should be targeted at a billion miles from Earth, roughly two years before the Golden Phoenix collides with Earth," Joe said.

"How big is the zone that each of these spacecrafts would be looking at, when it reaches its assigned point?" I asked.

"Each would be looking at a spherical cap with a base's diameter of one hundred seventy-four thousand miles—a big area. That's why we need to improve the on board radars, laser beams, and sensors."

I wrote the figures on my note pad. "Too big," I said. "Why we don't try to do the interception at a shorter distance?"

"We ran through our computer model the seven hundred million miles interception point case. It reduced the spherical cap base's diameter to one hundred twenty-two thousand miles. Significantly better, but the second set of data would arrive on Earth only fifteen months ahead of impact time instead of two years."

I shook my head. "Not enough time for launching the fighting spaceships and waiting for them to reach the intersection point. Why we don't destroy the asteroid right then, instead of taking data?"

"We take the orbit's data with unmanned and relatively

cheap spacecrafts. They won't carry any weapon system capable of destroying the asteroid," Joe said. "As you can see in the video now appearing in one of your conference room monitors, each spacecraft serves as mother ship for a fleet of twelve microsatellites. Once in the target zone, the mother ship releases the microsatellites, as portrayed in the computer simulation. Their mission is to constantly search the cosmos with a multitude of sensors, including radar pulses and laser beams."

"Once we know its orbit, what do we do? How are we going to get rid of it?" I asked.

"That you must ask the military services. The Air Force in particular," Jack said. "The destruction of the Golden Phoenix is their responsibility."

"You're right. I need to schedule a meeting with the Pentagon's top brass. Dr. Szklaruk and Dr. Patterson, please be ready for this all important meeting. I'll try to set it up for Thursday, August nineteen. I'll let you know the exact time," I said. "Gentlemen, I look forward to met you in person. Thank you all very much."

Jack stood and turned to me. "Are you ready to inspect your office space now?"

"Yes."

On our way there, I mentioned that I was going to hire a press deputy. Jack suggested several NASA people. I told him I had someone in mind, a personal friend for many years. I said, "I going to offer the position to my friend Rafi Sanchez."

He ushered me into the area assigned to my agency. Apparently, the people that worked there before left in a hurry because it was in total disarray. I walked toward the eastern most boundary of the room, where all the windows and private offices were, with the largest office on the southeast corner of the floor. Quickly, I decided this would be my office. I glanced around the empty room and said, "Jack, I'm going stay here for a little while. I hate to waste your time, so I'll get back to you later today, or early tomorrow."

Jack nodded. "I understand, take all the time you want."

After he left, I checked out the telecommunication computer system. Luckily, it was working. I contacted the human resources department, and requested a list of the employees assigned to work at NATA's office. The employment specialist who handled my request explained to me how to get the list out of my computer. I requested her to notify all employees to report to work on Wednesday morning, August 18, 2077, in room 807 at 7:30 sharp.

I walked around the area, asking myself: How I am going to organize this mess? I returned to my office and called Rafi. "My friend, I have an offer that you can't refuse."

"Where are you, big shot?"

"In Washington D.C.—Where else?" I sat down on the sole chair in the room.

"I heard that the President appointed you to head a new federal agency."

"I'm the Administrator of the National Asteroid Threat Administration."

"I knew it. What's up?"

"I need you here. I want you to be my Media Deputy. You're perfect for the position, with the right background and experience. Besides, I trust you. And that's a very important qualification in my book. It'll be a good launching pad for your political career."

"What career?" Rafi's voice trailed off.

"Come on, this is me you're talking to. I know that you want to run for public office. What do you say?"

"I'm in. But I need to give New Era some time to find a replacement for me."

"Huh-uh. Your planet needs you here tomorrow morning."

"Are you serious?"

"Dead serious." I hoped he'd noticed the somber tone of my voice.

"Okay, I'll see what I can do."

"So, you'll here tomorrow morning?"

"Have I ever let you down?"

"Good—I'll see you tomorrow."

"Wait .... Tell me where."

"Sorry, I forgot. NASA's national headquarters building in D.C., room 807."

That evening when I stepped into my apartment, I had the feeling that everything was all right with life. I knew my love was there and that she would be happy to see me. A superb homemaker, Jenny had transformed the bare apartment into a love nest. The contrast with Washington turmoil elated me. When she heard me opening the front door, she rushed to the entrance and kissed me passionately. She wore a white silky negligee. Taking my right hand, she led me to the living room and made me lie on a big couch, then proceeded to undress me slowly and tenderly.

With just my shorts on she massaged my neck and shoulders. "Close your eyes and relax." She pushed all the right buttons. I felt her fingers caressing my temples. Next, she put her index finger on the bridge of my nose and slid it down the middle of my body, following the contour of my penis. Holding my balls, she seemed to weigh them in her right hand. I pulled her toward me and laid her flat on the couch, looking up. She opened her legs. "Give it to me!" She shouted. I aimed my penis, grabbed her breasts, and pushed in as far it could go. I mumbled incoherent words without thinking, the animal libido within my brain was in total control. I could have dropped dead and died happy.

I spurted my semen and my soul into her. She took everything out of me. As I lay completely sated, she said, "Thank for the roses, my darling."

Later, with nothing else to give or say, I asked, "Where did you get this couch?"

She snuggled close to me. "I bought it, along with a couple other things, in a shop at Georgetown Pike."

"That was a quick delivery."

"I bought them on the condition of immediate delivery." She sounded like a petulant child.

"Good. We sure needed some furniture right away."

"I forgot, a man called you."

"What did he want?"

"I don't know. He just asked if this was your home."

"Did he leave any message?"

"No, he switched me off."

"Home keeper this is your new master."

"Yes, I recognize your voice patterns master from the reset you did the day you rented this apartment."

"Who called me today?"

"You had one caller."

"HK, identify caller," I commanded.

"Not possible. He erased his calling protocol, and the content of the communication. There is no way to trace that call. All I have is the time he went off the network."

"Okay, give me the time."

"2:47 P.M., August 17, 2077."

Jenny realized that I was disappointed. "What's wrong?" she asked.

"Honey, I don't like this a bit. We need to be very careful. We're living in a dangerous era—many people are becoming irrational and unstable because of the asteroid threat. Desperate people are capable of anything."

"What can we do?"

"I need to protect you. I'd rather die than let anything happen to you."

Before going out to eat, I took a shower and put on fresh, comfortable clothes. On the way to the restaurant and during dinner, I shared with Jenny all the things that happened in my first day at work.

"Does the President have any objection to our relationship?"

"No, I don't think so. I told him that I'm going to marry

you. Baby, would you please remind me, before I leave for work tomorrow morning, to order another dozen of red roses for you."

Jenny looked at me in disbelief. In mock indignation she retorted, "Don't even think about it, Mr. Tellez. You must save *something* for the project."

17 Kidnapping

I tried to meet with the Secretary of Defense and the Joint Chiefs of Staff on Thursday the nineteenth, but the brass objected to such short notice. We agreed to hold the meeting on Friday, August 27, at nine o'clock, at the Pentagon. Subsequently, I called the movers and advised them that I would be in San Antonio on the thirtieth instead of the twenty-fourth as we had agreed on before.

The original Pentagon was build in the 1940's during World War II. It was a massive single building which covered an area of twenty-nine acres of land, not counting the center court, and the huge parking lots. For many decades, the military establishment had opposed any suggestion to replace the obsolete building. They hated the old building but loved its excellent location on the Virginia side of the Potomac river, very close to National Airport and encircled by Interstate Highway 395, Jefferson Davis Highway, and Arlington National Cemetery. Above all, it was near the White House and the U.S. Capitol, close to the boss and the money appropriations, and, therefore irreplaceable.

On 2020, the old building was demolished and replaced by an state of the art military complex on the same location. The name, however, remained the same. The new Pentagon was the first dome enclosed building complex in the Washington D.C. area. The complex's environment was totally controlled: free of ultraviolet radiation, dust, rain, snow, and hydrocarbon gases and vapors. It consisted of a central building housing the Secretary of Defense and the Joint Chiefs of Staff offices, surrounded by four other identical buildings, one for each of the military services: Army, Navy, Air Force, and Marines.

At 8:45 Friday morning our aircraft landed on the visitors' area of the Pentagon's central building. There were four people in our party: Joe Szklaruk, Bob Patterson, Rafi, and myself. A Navy Captain and a civilian security officer escorted us to an office where they tagged us with visitor's passes. We rode an elevator to the fifth underground level where the conference room was situated. Once there, before entering the meeting place, we signed the logbook. A big rectangular table in the middle of the room reflected the rigid military hierarchical attitude prevalent at the highest level of the U.S. military establishment. The big table was surrounded by three rows of chairs. Our names were already on the table in front of our assigned chairs, on the left side, at the center of the table. The two outside rows of chairs on the right side of the table were already occupied by military officers and civilian personnel of the military services. A couple of minutes passed before the four Chiefs of Staff entered the room. The military personnel rose to their feet and sat again after the Chiefs sat, two at each side of the center chair on the right side of the table. Finally, the Secretary of Defense entered the room and sat on the center chair directly across the table from us. The military officers repeated the well choreographed routine.

Robert Randall, the secretary of defense, shook hands with each of us. He made eye contact with me, smiled halfheartedly, and said, "Mr. Tellez you requested the meeting. What can we do for you?"

I took a deep breath, instinctively shifted in my chair, and intentionally, for a couple of seconds, gazed back at the military faces piercing my skull with their concentrated stare. Unflappable, I replied, "Save our planet, sir."

The Secretary looked at me with keen eyes, "Save our planet from what?"

"From total destruction, sir," I dare to said.

"You need to be more specific, sir," he said tersely, narrowing his eyes.

"Of course. We put together a presentation for this meeting that I'd like to deliver now."

"Please, go ahead," said Robert Randall.

I opened my briefcase, pulled out a CD and handed it to a Navy officer, who inserted it into a computer. I walked to the podium in front of the north end of the table and, with the help of the superb video put together by NASA, explained to the Secretary of Defense and the Pentagon's brass what we knew about the Golden Phoenix.

I was surprised by the reaction of the Chiefs of Staff to my presentation. They expressed concern but remained calm and detached. The Secretary of Defense's demeanor differed drastically; he was astonished.

I decided to make the best I could of a bad situation. "I realize the threat is sixty-six years in the future and therefore somebody else's problem. I know we aren't going to solve this problem. But we must make sure that our descendants have the right weapons to solve it."

"What will happen if the Golden Phoenix collides with our planet?" the Secretary of Defense asked.

"I'm glad you asked that question, but I'll let Dr. Szklaruk answer it. He is truly an expert on the subject."

Joe stood up, and slowly walked to the podium. Once there, he combed his black bushy hair with both hands. He obviously was searching for the best way to start his presentation. He said:

"More than two-thirds of our planet's surface is covered by water. Therefore, it's probable that the asteroid will strike at one of the Earth's oceans. We think that the oceans are very deep, but they aren't. The Earth resembles a wet basket ball, indeed the ocean average depth is roughly 2.3 miles, which is insignificant when compared to the Earth's diameter of 7928 miles. The point is, we can't count on the ocean's water to absorb the impact of a rock that is 4.8 times larger than the ocean's depth, and which is traveling a 75,000 miles per hour. All the kinetic energy of the rock will be released at the instant of the impact. This huge amount of energy, millions of times larger than the energy released by all the atomic bombs exploded in our planet, will create a crater 200 miles in diameter and one mile deep. All the matter contained within this huge crater will be instantaneously converted into extremely high-temperature gases. The quick expansion of these superheated gases will produce a giant explosion that will propagate at supersonic speed in all directions annihilating everything in its path. It will travel several times around the world burning forest, destroying cities and killing billions of peoples. This will be closely followed, by a colossal tidal wave—a giant tsunami—that will smash against the shore line producing enormous destruction. The initial impact will strip away part of the Earth's atmosphere and push the planet out of its orbit by one hundred feet. It will also crack the Earth's crust at the bottom of the ocean and punch a hole right through the lithosphere and the Asthenosphere layers and will reach the molten magma in the mantel below. The collision will trigger a multitude of huge earthquakes as continental plates crash against each others. Ten thousand cubic miles of sea water will plunge into the huge pit of molten rock quenching it and creating a new crust. The resulting scar will be more than a hundred miles long and the vaporized water, very possibly contaminated with corrosive acids, will form immense cloud formations completely covering the Earth for years.

"The intense heat produced by the initial shockwave will be followed by a "rain of fire" in the form of hot particles reentering what is left of the Earth atmosphere after being thrown into space by the asteroid's impact. The rain of fire will last several hours and together with the monstrous fires ignited by the initial blast will create an oven-like environment that will kill most of the land based species in the planet, by roasting them alive.

"The collision with the Golden Phoenix will not only produce colossal devastation the day of the event, it'll also cover the Earth with a lid of water vapor and dust that the sun light can't penetrate. The Earth's surface will cool down and remain frozen for years. The surface temperature will eventually increase again, after the dust settle and the sky clears. But the unthinkable punishment won't stop there. The still large proportion of water vapor remaining in the atmosphere plus the carbon dioxide and ozone released during the fiery inferno will cause an atrocious greenhouse effect that will warm up the Earth's surface by preventing the escape of the infrared radiation—heat—to space. So, after the long, cold period of darkness the Earth will become very hot!

"Very few species will survive this combination of catastrophes. Ninety percent of all the species, on land and in the oceans, will be wiped out. The more adapted and well established in his ecological niche an species is, the quicker it will disappear. The human species will be one of the first to go. The surviving species will inherit the world and they will evolve in unpredictable ways."

Joe remained silent for a few seconds, watching the doomsday simulation on a large computer monitor behind the podium. "Hard to believe that this could really happen."

"No. It won't happen. We'll blow it up before it hits us," declared General Clayborne, the Army Chief of Staff. "Tell me, Dr. Szklaruk, what will happen if the asteroid hits land instead of the ocean?"

"Our computer model shows no big differences regardless of where the Golden Phoenix hits. If it directly hits ground, the cloud cover would contain more dust and would produce less acid rain. The initial shock wave would be larger, the earthquakes would be more intense, and they would produce more lava flows. Actually, it's a trade off, because the asteroid's kinetic energy must be dissipated one way or the other."

"How confident are you in your predictions?" Secretary Randall asked.

"Very confident, Mr. Secretary. We aren't working in a vacuum. Events like the one that I just described have happened before. Our planet has been hit many times by huge asteroids and comets. We know in great detail, that sixty-five million years ago a large object, six miles across, possible a portion of the nucleus of a comet, hit the shallow waters of the Gulf of Mexico, in what is now Puerto Chicxulub, a village on the western side of the tip of the Yucatan peninsula (which at the time was still submerged) in Mexico. It wiped out seventy percent of all the plant and animal species living at the time, dinosaurs included. This event changed forever the planet Earth. In fact, the human species evolved from the small mammals which survived that collision.

"Son, you have managed to scare us real well," General Clayborne said. "How do you plan to shoot it down?"

Joe paused, made eye contact with the imposing general, and calmly retorted, " General, I'm not your son."

The face of General Clayborne turned beet-red. He was on the verge of detonating. I could see him struggling to put a lid on his bad temper. He made a long and intimidating eye contact with Dr. Szklaruk. Finally he said: "Don't get cute with me, Joe."

I admired the courage of Dr. Szklaruk immensely. But I couldn't afford to let my first important meeting, as the NATA Administrator, to become a fiasco. Before Joe could answer the General's bullying and condescending statement, I raised my voice and said, "Gentlemen, I don't want to jeopardize this meeting. We're highly educated and very well paid public servants. I think that it would be a shame for us to waste our time bickering, when our country and future generations of Americans need the best of us. We are here to solve a problem, not to bicker with one another."

"Mr. Tellez, you're absolutely right. Let's have an early lunch break, and when we return, I want full cooperation from all present, nothing else," Declared the Secretary of Defense.

I opened the afternoon session. "I requested this meeting because we believe that it's the responsibility of the military services to destroy the Golden Phoenix. We can give you data and advice, and we can help you to plan this very difficult mission. But you'll be doing the shooting."

General James T. Russ, the Air Force Chief of Staff, asked, "How far in advance do you think we should intercept and destroy the asteroid?"

"The sooner the better, no less than one year before collision time. The exact point and time of interception depends of number of spaceships available and their capabilities."

The General's question broke the tension and set the tone of the afternoon session. Soon after that, all the military people attending the meeting began asking questions and voicing their opinions. I was happy to see everybody working together. I let Bob Patterson and Joe answer most of the questions.

After everyone got familiar with the requirements and the magnitude of the problem. General Russ said:

"The spacecraft we have now days are not good enough for this mission. We need to develop a new class of spaceships. They must be faster, more maneuverable, and have a much longer range. Actually, we need to discover a new means of propulsion. Our present day nuclear engines are too heavy and bulky."

"We have a contract with M.I.T. for long range technology forecasting. They claim that it's feasible to build a proton engine good enough for intergalactic travel. They're talking about speeds close to the speed of light," said Admiral Blakenship, the Navy Chief of Staff.

"How does it work?" Dr. Patterson asked.

"I don't know, but I believe it works by converting protons into pure radiation, that is, converting the protons' matter into energy," answered the Admiral.

"Another major problem is that the human body is incapable of resisting accelerations larger than two g's for long period of times. We must improve our present day systems for nullifying the effect of acceleration on the human body," argued General Russ.

As soon as General Russ finished his statement, Dr. Szklaruk said, "NASA is developing a 'Comfort Zone' for space travelers. They envision that future generations of spaceships will contain a built-in comfort zone inside which humans can travel in comfort while the spaceship is accelerating at ten g's."

"Exactly what we need," said General Russ.

General Clayborne, who'd been silent since the lunch break, huddled with two of his high ranking officers in the second row. He turned around and said, "To shoot down this fast moving and very large asteroid we need a weapon system that we don't have presently. Laser beams are not powerful enough. We could use nuclear tipped missiles, but we would need to carry many of them aboard each spaceship, and they are too heavy. I think we should develop a new kind of weapon system. I am thinking about antiquark guns."

"And what will be the advantage of using antiquark guns?" Robert Randall asked.

"Galactic Gunners, a corporation based in Austin, Texas, claims that this weapon system is the optimum weapon. It shoots rays of deadly antiquark particles in three different anticolors: antired, antigreen, and antiblue. These pencil-thin rays trigger an explosion within the target's matter. The target itself is the bomb! Anything containing quarks is potentially a bomb. And everything that we know or see contains quarks, the most basic ingredient of matter. The beauty of this weapon is that isn't heavy and bulky, yet is more destructive that anything else in nature."

"Is that a fact or a fantasy?" asked Secretary Randall.

Some years ago when I was doing theoretical research about "matter-free space channels" at the Austin's elementary particle accelerator I became familiar with the basic research carried out by Galactic Gunners, so before General Clayborne could answer I intervened. "It's no fantasy. It's theoretically possible, and technically feasible. I'm familiar with Galactic Gunners' work."

"I like that idea a lot. But to be sure, I'm going to let one of the 'Beltway Bandits' do a feasibility study about that weapon system," said Secretary Randall.

The meeting was ending, yet I didn't have any commitment from any of the military services. So I pressed for concrete results. "Gentlemen, the discussion has been very enlightening. Now we need to sort out who's going to do what."

The Secretary of Defense gave me a glacial look. As host and meeting chairman, he evidently thought that I was infringing upon his area of responsibility. He said, "Mr. Tellez, you must realize that we are talking about a project that will cost several trillion dollars."

"I do. But money isn't an object. We must do it, and doesn't matter how much it costs."

"Who says?"

"Common sense, and the President."

The people in the conference room, high ranking military officers and civilian executives, tried to contain their joy, but the grin and suddenly found joviality give them away. Money, big amounts of it, is the real Holy Grail of the Pentagon's worshipers.

Looking belligerent and dictatorial, the Secretary of Defense scrutinized the face of everyone seated at the table. After searching his personal notes, he assigned areas of responsibilities and action items to his people. Finally, displaying as much authority as he could, he said, "We'll reconvene in four weeks. In the meantime, each of the armed services must prepare cost estimates for budget purposes and preliminary program schedules. Mr. Tellez, you must assign liaison personnel to work very closely with us. Gentlemen, this meeting is adjourned."

We flew back to the building housing NASA's headquarters. We arrived there at 4:37 P.M., too late to go back to work. I went directly to the parking garage and drove home. I looked forward to another lovely evening with Jenny. When I opened my apartment's front door, I prepared myself for one of Jenny's surprises; instead I found a dark, empty room. Alarmed, I called her name several times, each time louder. The lack of response terrified me. In panic I started to search the apartment, then I heard the computer calling me, *"Master, I have a message for you."*

I rushed into the living room, where the main monitor was. "HK! Deliver the message."

The image of a big man wearing a ski mask appeared on the monitor. He said, *"Mr. Tellez, we got your girlfriend. If you want her back, you must follow our instructions and do what you are told. If you don't comply with our demands we'll kill her...."* The man kept talking but I wasn't listening. Panic overcame me, my legs became heavy. I couldn't move. I was frozen, petrified. The only thing working inside my body was my heart, which pounded in my chest at a fierce rate. It was working hard trying to bring me back to life. I slumped on the couch. Sweat dripping from my face, I took off my jacket and unbuttoned my shirt. “Home Keeper, repeat the message,” I shouted to the computer.

“....We can’t let the Mayan’s witches control our destiny. We want to go inside the Sacred Cenote and bring out all the witches. We’ll interrogate them right here in San Antonio, Texas. This is what we want from you. Don’t tell anyone that your girlfriend has been kidnaped. Don’t call the police or the FBI. Tomorrow, Saturday the 28th of August, be at your apartment in San Antonio. Wait there for our call.”

When the computer finished playing the message, I picked up the flower vase that had come with the roses that I gave to Jenny and threw it against the monitor.

“Master, why are you punishing me? I didn’t do anything wrong”

“Shut up...stupid dummy! Call Rafael Fuentes. He’s at the Marriott Residence Inn in Crystal City.”

“*Go ahead, master.”*

“Rafi, I must talk with you immediately.”

“I just arrived home. Can you wait until tomorrow?”

“No! It’s very important. Stay there I’m coming to see you.”

“You’re determined to spoil my first Friday night in Washington. Okay, come over.”

At 5:45 the traffic was still heavy. It took me almost an hour to reach Crystal City. Rafi had just taken a shower and was enjoying Scotch on the rocks when I arrived.

“What happened?” he asked

“They kidnaped Jenny.”

Rafi’s face froze. “Who?”

“I don’t know. They want me to help them capture the

Itzaes. They'll kill Jenny if I don't collaborate with them. I must be in San Antonio tomorrow."

"Did you call the police?" Rafi asked as he put his drink down.

"No. They specifically told me not to. They said that they would kill Jenny if I do. In fact, I'm not suppose to be telling this to you."

"What do you want me to do?"

"I am leaving for San Antonio early tomorrow morning. I want you to contact the FBI and inform them of what happened. Explain to them that Jenny's life is in jeopardy if I speak with them. Then call the President in my name and tell him about it. Don't confide in any staff member, tell that only to the President, not anyone else. I'll be in touch with you. In the meantime, please try to conceive a rescue plan. My mind is not working now. I need your help."

Rafi nodded, leaned back in the chair, and as we gazed at each other he said, "My friend, I feel sorry for you. What else could happen to you? I'll help you in anyway I can."

"Thank you, I knew I could count with you. I need to leave now. I'm going to get ready for tomorrow."

"Tito, don't try to be a hero. Let the FBI handle this situation, it's their job. They're expert on this kind of thing."

"You're right, but I need to do something. I love her, she's my everything. I'm ready for action."

Back in my apartment, I called Ruben and explained to him that something terrible had happened, but that I couldn't tell him over the computer lines. He agreed to meet me at 8:20 A.M. at the transcontinental shuttle station in San Antonio.

18 The Ambush

Ruben and I went directly from the shuttle station to my apartment on the seventeenth floor of the Golden Tortilla complex. After searching the apartment completely, I said, "Let's go down to the atrium. This apartment may be bugged."

Ruben nodded. "That's fine with me."

We rode the elevator to ground level and once in the giant atrium, we crossed to the other side. We ordered a couple of large espressos at the coffee parlor near the north entrance of the complex and sat to talk. "Ruben what I'm about to reveal to you is a life or death secret, literally, and you must not disclose it to anyone."

Without losing eye contact, Ruben took a sip of his coffee, and said, "Tito you've known me for many years, and we're very good friends. Whatever it is I won't tell anyone."

"They kidnapped Jenny."

"Who?"

"I don't know. I was hoping you could tell me."

I contacted Ruben because he was an independent thinker, and extremely well informed. He shook his head. "Me? I don't know anything about it."

"I know that. But perhaps you have an idea of who would do such a thing."

Ruben smiled and said, "For sure, they're radical people who will stop in nothing. They distrust the government, and have their own agenda. I guess the kidnappers are connected with the extreme right. And you know how strong they are in Texas. They could be involved in the assassination of the Texas Governor."

"Thank you, my friend. I appreciate your comments. I need to go back to my apartment and wait for the perpetrators to contact me, as they said they would."

Ruben looked around, suspiciously, took a little metal box out of his jacket pocket and handed it to me. Almost imperceptibly he said, "You may need this. It contains twelve miniature hand grenades. Powerful stuff. Keep them dry. Don't forget, contact me if you need anything else."

I looked at my watch. It was 12:35 P.M. I stood up and went back to my apartment. Once inside, I encountered two intruders wearing ski masks. One of them pointed a laser gun at me, while the other searched me. He found and opened the little box containing the miniature hand grenades. "What's this?"

"My medicine. I have a heart condition."

"What condition?"

"Angina."

"Oh yeah? Go ahead and swallow one."

"No! that would kill me. I take those pills as a last recourse, only if I am having a heart attack."

He closed the "pill box" and handed it back to me.

The guy with the laser gun said, "Let's go."

"Where?"

"To Mexico."

"I don't go anywhere without seeing Jenny first. Where is she?"

"Listen, buster, if you don't cooperate, we'll get rid of you and her," the guy with the laser gun said.

"Don't worry, man, she is already there," said the first masked man, the one that searched me.

They pushed me out of the apartment. We walked to the end of the corridor and climbed the fire stairs all the way up to the the twenty-second level. From there, we climbed narrow metal stairs to the roof. Once on the roof, they took off their oversized jackets. Both men were fitted with a rocket harnesses. Grabbing and holding me, they fired the small rockets attached to the harnesses, and jumped. We landed on the service area of the complex. They gagged and pushed me into a white commercial van. Once inside the van I was blindfolded. We left the complex by the service entrance.

We drove about twenty minutes before we stopped. We entered a building, someone said, "Take him upstairs. The Boss is waiting."

We walked forty steps, and climbed two flights of a metal stairs. I concluded that the building was a warehouse, or something similar. We seemed to enter a room where they made me sit down. Then, they took off the blindfold and the gag. A very bright light was shining directly in my eyes.

“Turn off the damn light. I can’t see,” I shouted.

“That’s the idea,” said a new voice. I concluded it was the Boss’ voice.

“This is what we want you to do...”

“I do nothing with the light on.”

I couldn’t make out the conversation, but I heard the Boss talking with two or three other men. Finally, the light went off. It was a big room, almost empty. A big man stood in front of me. He grabbed my shirt and picked me up and before I could do or say anything, he punched me in my left eye. I fell against the wall. He grabbed me, and just before hitting me again, he said, “I work for the FBI. Go along with me, hit me back.”

I hit him on the chin, and he felt the sting of my punch. He wrapped his left arm around my neck and squeezed. He hit me repeatedly with his right fist in the stomach while saying, “We are going to switch cenotes. The Itzaes are really Mexican Federales. They must deliver Jenny before you do anything. We suspect they also assassinated the Texas governor.”

He knocked me out with a hard blow to my chin. I fell to the floor. I heard the others come into the room. One of them said, “Hey, man, don’t kill him.”

When I tried to stand up, I stumbled. One of them grabbed me and said, “What’s it gonna be? You feel talking now?”

“Yeah.”

“We leave for Mexico tonight. Don’t try anything. You must cooperate with us, especially when we arrive in Mexico. You must appear to be an American tourist. A happy American tourist, " said the Boss.

"Where in Mexico are we going?"

"Are you a sarcastic asshole or what?" The Boss looked at me with piercing eyes. "We'll land in Cancun. And you must act naturally, as if nothing's wrong with you. Understand?"

"Yes, sir."

I was taken to a smaller room by the same two men that picked me up at my apartment. They locked the door. Before leaving, they said, "Go ahead and take a shower. We want you to look like a happy tourist."

I was glad the door was locked. Finally, I was alone. In my mind, I went over what the big guy told me. Apparently, the FBI planned to take these guys to a different cenote. An excellent idea, because they didn't know which one of the many cenotes in the area was the Sacred Cenote. The problem was that I didn't know where to take them. I didn't know which one of the cenotes was the phony one—the one that the FBI and the Mexican Federales had secured, staged and surrounded. I kept thinking, even while in the shower, about all the possibilities. I concluded that the FBI, the Mexican Federales, and whoever else was involved in this rescue mission must know that I didn't know where the phony Sacred Cenote is. Therefore, I reasoned, they intended to pass that information to me, and I must be ready for it.

At 7:50 P.M. the same two men came into the room. One of them said, "Time to move out, buddy. Let's go."

We walked out of the building, that now, I realized, was a

hangar. We boarded a plane parked outside. The Boss and the FBI undercover agent were already inside the jet and the Boss was talking with the pilot. He turned around and barked some instructions to the FBI agent, who immediately exited the plane. I saw him running toward the hangar.

Two hours later, at 10:50 P.M. local time, we landed in Cancun. I heard the pilot speaking in Spanish to the control tower. He was instructed to take the plane to an area reserved by customs for arriving private planes. The pilot taxied the plane, and stopped it in front of a long building.

A Mexican custom agent came out to meet us. "[How many in your party, Mr. Maxwell?]"

"[Five.]"

"[Grab your luggage and follow me.]"

I didn't have any luggage. Each of the perpetrators carried a small, black suit case. We walked fast to keep pace with the Mexican agent. We came to a large room with a couple of custom stations.

The custom agent stopped in the middle of the room, turned around and faced us. He shouted, "[Each of you must fill out a custom's declaration. You will find them on top of the counter on your left.]"

The two enforcers were having a terrible time filling out the form. Finally, the Boss and the pilot did it for them.

"[Hey you!]" yelled another custom agent. He gestured for me to approach his station. "[Over here.]"

When I reached his station, I could not believe my eyes. It was Ramon. I handed the form to him.

"[Where is your I.D.?]"

I handed him my driver's license. He looked at it with faked interest.

"[Mr. Tellez, if you plan to drive you must obey all the signs.]" He gave me a piercing look.

"[Understood, sir,]" I replied while returning the piercing look. "[But, could you be more specific?]"

"[Unless you're blind, you can't miss them. Follow the signs for the Sacred Cenote.]"

He stamped a little piece of paper with the time and arrival date, 11:10 P.M., Saturday, 28 August 2077. "This is your admission document. You must bring it back when you are ready to leave." Nonchalant he shouted, "Next!"

I walked away from the custom's station and stopped in the corridor to wait for the others. I thought it had been a neat way to pass me the information I needed. After a short while, the others joined me. I pondered where they might have hidden their weapons. We exited the building without incident. The pilot called a taxi, and in fluent Spanish, he told the driver where to go.

The taxi driver wasn't in a hurry, an unheard of occurrence in Cancun. It took him fifty minutes to get us to our destination. It was 12:05 A.M. when we arrived at a two story house in a residential section of town, not too far away from the strip where all the big hotels were. A black car was parked in the driveway.

Inside the house, the Boss said, "Aren't you glad to be in your native country?"

"This isn't my country. More than ten generations of my family were born in Texas. But I'm glad to be here," I said.

The Boss shook his head, gave me a scornful look. "Sure, all the Chicanos say the same thing. I don't trust any of you."

"It's true, whether you believe it or not. You can read about it in any history book. The only ones that had been around longer than us are the pure native Americans. I don't trust you either, Mr. Maxwell."

When I mentioned his name, he became enraged. He pushed me against the wall, grabbed my shirt, and said, "You will never be one of us. You aren't American, you're a fucking Mexican. Nothing but dirt. Alex! Get this old mother fucker out of here before I kill him. Lock him in his room."

On my way out, I shouted, "Where's Jenny? I must see her before I take you to see the Itzaes."

The next morning, Alex woke me up and took me down to the kitchen. I drank some coffee and ate a soggy Mexican muffin. It was 7:10 A.M. on the kitchen clock. "Get ready. We're leaving in ten minutes," Alex said.

"I won't go anywhere without Jenny."

"She's coming with us. You will see her before we leave."

I went to the upstairs bathroom. I couldn't shave, but urinated and washed my hands and face. Finally, I checked to see if the pill box was still in my jacket's pocket. From the bathroom's window I had a commanding view of the front yard and driveway. As I left the bathroom, a car drove in. The two rear doors opened. A man stepped out of the car on the left side and Jenny stepped out of the car on the right side. The driver joined them as they walked toward the front door. My heart raced, and I was happy to see her alive, but I thought it was odd how they came out of the car.

Five minutes later, they escorted me out of the house and into the black car. Maxwell and Alex sat with me on the back seat. The other enforcer sat in the driver seat. Then, I saw Jenny again. She and the two men came out of the house and back to their car. No question about it. It was her! I must have smiled, because the Boss said, "Are you satisfied, Mr. Tellez?"

I tried not to show my happiness, "I'd like to see her more closely."

"Come on, Mr. Tellez, don't play games with me. That's Jenny, and you know it," Maxwell said.

"I won't take you to the Sacred Cenote until you release Jenny."

Maxwell eyes narrowed. "If you don't take us to the Sacred Cenote and arrange a meeting with the Itzaes, you won't see her alive again."

"I'll take you there, but I won't arrange the meeting until you release Jenny."

He paused, his expression became thoughtful. Finally he said, "Okay."

We arrived at Chichen Itza at 9:55 Sunday morning. The archaeological site, usually a busy place full of tourists, was deserted. As soon as we parked, Maxwell opened the car's trunk and handed out weapons to the members of his gang. He gave me an intimidating look and said, "Take me to the Sacred Cenote."

"We must start at the Castle. It's the only way I know how to reach the Sacred Cenote. "

"Where's the Castle?" Maxwell asked.

"Over there, in the middle of the esplanade. It's the tallest structure in the complex."

"That's a pyramid not a castle," Maxwell said.

"I know. That's what the Mayans called it."

Maxwell waved to his accomplices in the second car and told them to follow us. I saw Jenny with them. We walked about seven hundred feet to reach the Castle, a short distance in normal conditions, but it was extremely hot and humid, so everybody was tired and sweating profusely by the time we reached the base of the Castle—especially the perpetrators who carried heavy laser guns. The Castle was a four sided structure with a long flight of narrow steps in the middle of each side leading to the temple on the top. It was about one hundred feet high and two hundred feet on each side of the base.

Eight trails connected the Castle to the the other buildings and monuments in the complex. They were ancient trails paved with time-rounded rocks. Looking for signs, I walked around the base of the Castle. On the south side, I found a large arrow-shaped sign. "To the Sacred Cenote," it said.

We followed the trail indicated by the sign. Jenny's group walked fifty feet behind. The trees and bushes lining both sides of the trail were ugly, dusty, and wind beaten. The strange vegetation, the unsettling silence, and the prevailing sticky calm, gave the place an aura of surrealism. The landscape reminded me of Salvador Dali's paintings. I thought I was dreaming. Further down the trail we encountered a second sign, it read: 600 feet to the Sacred Cenote. Maxwell readied his weapon and the others did the same. I was dripping wet with sweat. As we approached the 'Sacred Cenote,' I looked around trying to figure out what the set up was. I didn't see anything. Then I looked in the direction of the second group. I recognized Jenny's dress.

Maxwell saw the cenote first. "Stop—everybody stop," he shouted. He looked through his laser gun's sight in the direction of the cenote. "The trail forks around the cenote. I can see a shed at the edge of the cenote. Tellez, do you recognize that shed?"

"Yes, it was there before."

"Let's go real slow. Tellez, you go first," ordered Maxwell. "And don't forget Jenny is back there."

We stopped again at about ten feet from the cenote's edge. "Tellez, do your thing now. Go ahead and look for the Itzaes. We'll wait here," Maxwell said.

"No. You must deliver Jenny first. That was the agreement."

Maxwell expression darkened. A second later he rushed toward me. We stared at each other, his wide bullish face a millimeter from mine. The fact that I didn't blink made him madder. I felt hot air coming from his snout and experienced the intimidating gaze of his eyeballs which were congested with blood. I was mad as hell and afraid of nothing. Suddenly, he pushed me. I fell backward, and he aimed his laser gun at me. I'll never know if he was bluffing and trying to intimidate me. He was incinerated by the powerful rays of heavy laser guns. A piece of burnt flesh hit me on the chest; its pungent odor made me puke. Alex, who was standing next to Maxwell, turned around to respond to the attack. He was hit in the face. With his hair on fire, he screamed in excruciating pain. He fell dead with his mouth open. His eyes and nose were gone. The other enforcer ran toward the cenote and jumped. The rays from three laser guns got him in mid air. His charred body sizzled when it hit the water.

The battle lasted less than two minutes. Mexican Federales rushed to my side. I shouted, "[Jenny is with the other group.]"

I looked toward Jenny's group and saw smoke, then I heard someone shouting, "[They're all dead.]"

"[Stupid! Assassins! You killed her, too.]" I ran toward the second group.

When I reached the site of the ambush, a Mexican officer grabbed me. "[Mr. there is nothing to see, they're all dead. I'm sorry,]" He shook me.

I brushed him aside and walked toward the corpses. Jenny had fallen face down. She still held a hand gun. Her arms and legs were wide open. Apparently she was running toward the cenote when the laser ray had hit her in the back.

Tenderly, crying, in a trance I managed to turn her over. She wore a rubber mask.

Full of expectations and with renewed hope, I pulled off the rubber mask. It wasn't Jenny. My mood instantly changed from sorrowful to euphoric. "[It's not Jenny!]" I yelled to the troops surrounding me. Someone wearing an FBI jacket asked, "Do you recognize her?"

"No, I don't."

19 Jenny's Rescue

After the battle, three FBI agents and I rode back to Cancun. I told them how concerned I was for Jenny's safety. And that I was afraid the kidnapper would kill her immediately after learning about the ambush and the fate of their partners. One of the FBI agents explained that neither they nor the Mexican Federales would say anything to the media, but he was sure the news would leak out anyway.

Late that afternoon I checked into the Sheraton Hotel and reserved a seat on a commercial flight for my return trip to San Antonio early the next morning. I called Rafi and Ruben and told them about my ordeal in Chichen Itza, and that I was frightened by the possibility that the kidnappers would kill Jenny. I asked Rafi to inform the President.

Golden Tortilla Residential Complex
San Antonio, Texas
10:30 Monday morning, 30 August 2077.

Two men from South West Van Lines were waiting for me at the complex. I'd forgotten about them completely. "How long have you been waiting?"

"Since 10:15. We came to do the packing for you," said the older of the two men. He wore a cap with a peculiar emblem, It depicted a black horned-incubus at the center of a red five-pointed star. I had seen that emblem before but I couldn't remember where.

"Sorry, fellows. I had a terrible weekend."

"We know. We heard about your troubles down there in Cancun," said the younger guy.

"Really? Then, I guess by now everybody in Texas knows about it."

"Yeah, and you're lucky the referendum is tomorrow. Otherwise the media would be here interviewing you."

"Well, I'll get out of your way. I don't want to slow you down," I said.

"Sir, you need to tell me what items you want to put in storage."

We walked through the entire apartment. I pointed out what was supposed to go where. Before leaving them alone, I asked the older guy where they would store my furniture.

"In our warehouse right across the street from our office. It's near the intersection of I-37 and highway 181," he replied. "Here's my card. It has the complete address and phone number."

"Computer, let me talk with Ruben Vargas."

"Ruben I need your help."

"Where are you?" Ruben asked

"Right here in San Antonio."

"Great! I'm glad you made it all the way back in one piece."

"Where do you think they are hiding Jenny, if she is alive?"

"My friend, I hate to say this but that's a big if."

"I know, I know. Don't tell me that," I said. "This isn't preaching time, damn it."

"Sorry, man. Cool down, okay?"

"I'm desperate—help me, Ruben."

"Is it safe to talk?"

"The movers are in the kitchen packing my china. I'm in my office with the door locked. So it should be okay."

"Listen, the FBI, the Texas Rangers, and the San Antonio police are looking for Jenny. There is a country-wide alert in effect," Ruben said. "Actually, there is not much you can do, only wait."

"I can't do that. This thing is driving me crazy. Understand?" I shouted.

"She's probably here in San Antonio."

"Why?"

"They met with you here, and they took off for Mexico from here also," Ruben said. "Obviously, their power base is here in San Antonio. So their accomplices and hiding places are probably here also."

"That's brilliant my friend," I said. "I'm going to go out and look for her myself."

"Tito, remember that the Texas referendum is tomorrow."

"So what?"

"A large number of security forces are already in place, including the National Guard," replied Ruben. "Be careful. Don't do anything foolish."

"Thank you for the advice, my friend. I'll call you tomorrow."

I spent the rest of the day trying to find Jenny. Because they took me to a hangar before leaving for Cancun, I concentrated my efforts on civilian airports in the San Antonio metropolitan area. I disregarded the many air force bases located in the San Antonio area. My main targets were hangars and warehouses located in general aviation airfields. It was a waste of time. The only thing that I found was suspicious security guards. Everybody was interested in the referendum and nobody knew or cared about Jenny. At seven o'clock in the evening, dejected and tired, I returned to my apartment.

All our small items were packed in carton boxes. The movers had left a note for me. It said, "We'll be back on September, the second, at 9:00 A.M. to pick up the furniture and boxes."

The TV channels carried, almost exclusively, referendum propaganda, but my mind was busy thinking about Jenny and her whereabouts. I went to bed early. I had a terrible night on the bare sofa. Although I was very tired and emotionally drained, I fell sleep very late.

I went to vote at eleven o'clock in the morning. I was glad that the TV reporters stationed outside the precinct didn't recognize me. I visited the San Antonio FBI field office. The agent in charge explained that there was nothing new in their investigation. He mentioned that their lab was still working on the evidence recovered at the Chichen Itza crime site, and that the kidnapper corpses were on their way to San Antonio.

The 'I did everything I could' attitude was winning the battle inside my mind. I felt pessimistic and depressed. I returned home, took a three hour nap, and then a shower. I was getting ready to go out when I heard a commotion right outside my apartment door. Many of my neighbors were on their way out. Someone shouted at me, "Congratulations! We won!"

HemisFair Plaza
Downtown San Antonio
Eight o'clock in the evening
31 August 2077.

The victory party was absolute total chaos, but a happy chaos. Simultaneously, millions of people went temporarily crazy. A great number of them rode trucks, vans, car, or motorcycles. Others rode bikes, skated or just walked. All of them were yelling, hauling, and honking. Overwhelmed by the sheer number of people and moved by the genuine demonstration of patriotism, the police were nowhere in sight. Traffic regulations weren't enforced. They let the people celebrate their victory.

Suddenly, everyone was your friend. Strangers hugged or kissed each other. There were more losers (the independence proposition got fifty-nine percent of the votes) than winners. The remarkable thing was that both were enjoying the moment and having a great time.

Walking down Durango Street, which looked more like a parking lot than a street, I spotted a green truck with a rare bumper sticker. It depicted a black horned-incubus at the center of a red five-pointed star. Immediately, I realized that the truck bumper sticker was identical to a bumper sticker I saw on Jenny's husband's car some time back. It was also identical to the emblem on the mover's cap. Right then, I realized the movers were Jenny's husband's accomplices!

Luckily, I remembered the mover said their warehouse was near the intersection of I-37 and Highway 181. I ran five or six blocks to my car, which was parked near the Convention Center. I hopped into my car and drove toward Interstate 37. I took the southbound access ramp near the eastern boundary of HemisFair Plaza. The traffic was awful. Ten minutes later, I pulled off at the Highway 181 exit, and stopped my car in the parking lot of a gone-out-of-business store. I stepped out of my car and searched my pants and jacket pockets for the business card that the mover had given me. In the chest pocket of my jacket, I found the 'pill box' that Ruben gave me. I opened the little box and said to myself, "Beautiful! This is exactly what I need." I left the box open and put it back in my chest pocket. I kept looking for the business card. I found it in my wallet. Then, I took my Magnum 357 revolver from the glove compartment. It was inside the leather holster that I bought after the shooting on Pepe's boat. I strapped it, police detective's style, on my left side.

I looked around and realized that the South West Van Lines warehouse was in the next block. Before bolting for the warehouse, I called 911 and told the operator to alert the police and the FBI. Briefly, I explained to her what I intended to do.

Just before turning right onto the South West Van Lines office's parking lot, I switched off my car's head lights. With great care, I parked it with the front looking out.

The warehouse was right across the highway. The imminent threat of an approaching fight, triggered an avalanche of adrenal hormones inside my body. Suddenly, I became a fighting beast with the instincts of predator. I was ready for aggression.

Fearless, I crossed the highway and climbed the warehouse perimeter fence. The perimeter lights went on. I rushed to the building's entrance and knocked hard on the front door. Nothing happened. The door was firmly closed. Desperate, I backed off a step and crashed my shoulder into the door. To my surprise the door opened without resistance, and I found myself on the floor.

Before I could recover from the fall, a tall man rushed toward me and yanked out my revolver from the holster. "I always wanted to kill someone with one of these old revolvers," he said.

He made the fatal mistake of turning around and taking three or four steps before firing. It gave me time to grab a handful of miniature hand grenades and throw them at him. Simultaneously, I yelled: "Hey, you!"

The assassin turned around and instinctively fired at the grenades. One of the miniature grenades hit him on the forehead and exploded. The other three exploded a fraction of a second later when they hit the floor. He was decapitated and dismembered. I realized then that he was a cyborg. I recovered my gun and put it back in the holster.

I heard a woman yelling for help. It was Jenny's voice. I ran toward the opposite side of the warehouse's main bay. I came to a door. I kicked it open and entered a small room.

Jenny was there and so was Bob, her husband. "Watch out, he has a gun," she shouted.

"So do I." I pointed my gun at him.

Bob was a cunning coward, incapable of confronting another man. He had no sense of honor and no shame in lying. His favorite weapon was a lawsuit.

"Put down your gun or I'll kill you, bastard!" I shouted and cocked my revolver.

"Where is the cyborg?" Bob asked.

"I killed him," I answered.

My pants, jacket, even my socks were stained with the cyborg's blood. I looked like a butcher gone mad.

That was enough for him. "Don't shoot! Take Jenny, if that's what you want." He dropped his gun.

"You can't negotiate your way out of this one. No injunction, no subpoena will save you. This is payback time," I said. "Now it's between you and me. Mano-a-mano."

I put my revolver back in the holster, and got closer to him. In panic, instinctively, he shielded his face with his arms. I hit him with fury, several times. The first blow hit his open mouth, the second landed in his stomach, and the third glanced his left eye. He fell on his knees, bleeding profusely from his mouth. I was going to administer a second series of blows when I heard someone yell, "Freeze!"

I looked back and saw two police officers with their guns

pointing at me. I immediately stepped back and said, "I was the one that called you."

Jenny and I embraced. The ordeal was finally over.

More police officers and FBI agents arrived. Briefly, they interrogated us right there in the scene of the crime. After sorting things out, they escorted us downtown to the main police station. There, they interrogated us separately for more than an hour. Luckily, the media was busy analyzing the referendum results, so we left the police station quietly, without being harassed by the media.

20 Epilogue

The GF drug store at the Golden Tortilla Complex.

11:10 P.M., 31 August 2077.

"Mr. Tellez, what happened to you?" the clerk asked.

"It's a long story. Tomorrow you'll read about it in the newspapers," I said. "We each need two sets of underwear and pajamas."

"Isle seventeen in the rear."

"Do you have towels in the apartment?" Jenny asked.

"No, get a couple, and some soap and shampoo."

Riding the elevator to the apartment, thinking about what was coming, I became aroused.

"Cool down, my love. Don't spoil the moment. We both need to take a shower first."

"You're right, but you're excited, too."

"I'm so hot that I'm melting away," Jenny admitted.

"Boy! That's a big bottle of champagne. Are you sure you have enough?"

"All that you need, baby."

We both laughed. I loved her sense of humor.

Once inside the apartment we did not waste any time. She took off her shirt. I removed her bra and unzipped her pants. She stepped out of them and let them drop to the floor. All that remained was her panties.

"I'm so glad we're back together," I said, pulling off her panties.

I was on my knees when I tried to kiss her. "Take me to the shower," she said softly as she pulled back.

I lifted her and carried her to the shower. We let the water run as we lathered each other. I held her tightly and caressed her entire body. She stroked my upper back, tickling it with her fingernails. She reached downward and squeezed my penis. Our slippery bodies were moving in sync. In a frenzy, I raised her and lowered myself downward. In a single stroke I plugged her pussy hole. It was in the nick of time. I came, and she followed me right after.

We sat on the shower floor for a little while, then stood up and continued our shower. We had a second round, when I became aroused again while drying her lovely body. It was wonderful and lasted longer.

"How did you survive for so many days?" I asked.

Jenny hesitated for a second. "They raped me every day," she said with her voice trailing off.

"Who?"

She lowered her eyes then whispered, "All of them."

I was moved by her honesty and glad that she had the strength to bring it all out. "I'm glad they're all dead."

"Bob isn't dead."

"Yeah, but he doesn't count."

It was a painful admission. I opened the champagne bottle, and we drank until we fell asleep.

"Master, Ruben wants to talk with you."

"HK, I instructed you not to wake me up before nine."

"It's ten after nine, master."

"Put him on."

"Congratulations, old pal. You're six hundred thousand dollars richer."

"What are you talking about?"

"The cyborg you killed last night was the same one that killed the governor of Texas. My friend, you won a six hundred thousand dollar reward."

"Really? How did they know?"

"The microchip they recovered at the scene of the crime in Washington had one hundred, twenty-eight mechanical interfaces. They all matched perfectly with the interfaces of the cyborg that you killed last night."

"Are they sure?"

"A hundred percent sure. No question about."

"Yahoo—yahoo! God bless America! Jenny! Wake up, my darling, we hit the jackpot."

"Ruben, my friend, I'm so happy, that I can't think straight. Would you do me a favor?"

"Sure, what?"

"South Western Van lines is supposed to come tomorrow to

pick up our furniture. I don't want to have anything to do with those crooks. Would you cancel my contract with them and make arrangements with another company to move my belongings to Washington?"

"No problem. I'll take care of that for you. When are you leaving?"

"Today. Ruben, I appreciate very much what you've done for me."

"Tito, you're an exceptional man. I'm proud to be your friend. I'll see you in Washington."

The White House
Washington, D.C.
Monday 10:00 A.M., 6 September 2077.

The President received me in the Rose Garden. It was a splendid day, not a single cloud in the sky and the temperature was a balmy sixty-five degrees. The White House looked majestic. The President was happy and optimistic. The Rose Garden was the appropriate setting for a friendly conversation.

"Tito, my friend, for a while I thought I wouldn't see you again."

"You weren't alone. I thought so, too."

"You know what? I would have loved to have been there. In the middle of the gigantic outpouring of love for country and fellow citizens," the President said.

Mark took a small leather cigar case from his jacket pocket, opened it, and offered me a cigar. I placed it under my nose and sniffed hard. "This is a good one. Where did you get it?"

"It was a gift from the Cuban ambassador," the President

said. "He mentioned that it came from Falcon, a little town in the center of the island."

We lit up and leaned back in the lounge chairs, enjoying the exquisite taste of well-aged premium tobacco leafs, admiring the layered structure of the long white ash tip, and watching the rings of white smoke grow larger as they floated away. There's nothing like a good cigar to celebrate in peace and tranquility.

"We need to make sure this is a long-lasting victory," the President said. "We can't afford to go through another referendum a few years from now."

"You're absolutely right. That's why it's vital that we Latinos get a fair proportion of the power in this great nation of ours."

"Don't worry my friend. It'll happen," he said. "I hate to admit it, but Senator Santamarina could be the next President. Do you know if he has somebody in mind for Vice President?"

"Who knows? I think he's partial to Jack Zimmerman, the governor of New York. And with him in our ticket we'll get for sure the majority of the Jewish vote in the entire country."

Mark was a consummate politician, and he knew how to steer a conversation in the right direction. "I heard that you won a large reward for killing the cyborg that assassinated the Texas governor."

"True. I don't have the money yet. The San Antonio chief of police told me that I'd have to wait until the investigators complete their report."

For a little while we smoked our cigars in silence, lost momentarily in our owns thoughts. The President glanced beyond me, then nodded. I didn't want to appear rude, so I didn't turn around to find out who else was there. Apparently, he'd made eye contact with someone else, perhaps an aide.

"I have good news for you. Last Wednesday, the day after the referendum, I had a meeting with the leaders of the House and the Senate, and the Secretary of Defense. We discussed the Golden Phoenix threat and the funding required to shoot it down. We didn't discuss specific amounts of money because we don't have a plan yet. Although everybody understood that the program total cost would be in the trillions of dollars."

"Was the funding for NATA discussed?" I asked.

"Yes. I told them that we budgeted five billion dollars in fiscal year 2078 for NATA."

"Any objection?"

"No, although the Speaker of the House asked how we'd arrived at that number. I explained that it was an educated guess. Tito, you must provide the Budget Office with a detailed funding request for FY 2078. You only have a few days left before they print the 2078 budget book."

"Do you think the Congress will accept an addendum containing NATA's budget?"

"Yes, but that will give you only a couple of weeks more," replied the President. "The real problem is the budget for the Department of Defense. Bob Randall is counting with you and the Chiefs of Staff. He needs an estimate of the funding required for the Golden Phoenix project during fiscal year 2078."

"We're going to meet again on September 24. I'm sure after the meeting we'll know the real magnitude of the project much better," I said.

The President put the cigar on the ash tray and stood up. I did the same. We gazed at each other as he shook my hand. "Well my friend I'm glad to have you back on board. How is your girlfriend?"

"She's doing very well considering what she went through."

"When is the wedding?"

"Real soon. Now that her husband is in jail, her divorce should go very fast."

"Good bye, Tito."

"Good bye, Mark."

ORDERING INFORMATION

Do not send cash. Send your check or money order to:

Outer Space Press
P.O. Box 9593
Daytona Beach, FL 32120

	1 Copy	2 Copies
Hardcover	$20.95	$41.90
Shipping, postage, and handling charges (USA only)	0.00	0.00
Shipping, postage, and handling charges (Canada and Mexico)	4.00	6.00
For **priority** mailing (USA only), add	3.00	3.00
Florida residents, please add 6% sales tax.	1.26	2.51
Local sales tax, if any	-----	-----
Total	-----	-----

Make check payable to Outer Space Press.

Write in your order: Texas 2077 hardcover edition.

Provide your name and complete address.

Canada and Mexico residents must remit in U.S. currency. For shipping costs to any other country, contact the publisher.